YA
364.66 DEA
Brenner, Samuel.
The death penalty /
SUN 1074524651

WITHDRAWN

WORN, SOILED, OBSOLETE

The Death Penalty

Other books in the Issues on Trial series:

Civil Liberties and War
The Environment
Freedom of the Press
Individual Rights and the Police
Racial Discrimination
Reproductive Rights
Rights of the Accused
Students' Rights

The Death Penalty

Samuel Brenner, Book Editor

GREENHAVEN PRESS
An imprint of Thomson Gale, a part of The Thomson Corporation

Detroit • New York • San Francisco • San Diego • New Haven, Conn.
Waterville, Maine • London • Munich

Bonnie Szumski, *Publisher*
Helen Cothran, *Managing Editor*
Scott Barbour, *Series Editor*

© 2006 Thomson Gale, a part of The Thomson Corporation.

Thomson and Star Logo are trademarks and Gale and Greenhaven Press are registered trademarks used herein under license.

For more information, contact:
Greenhaven Press
27500 Drake Rd.
Farmington Hills, MI 48331-3535
Or you can visit our Internet site at http://www.gale.com

ALL RIGHTS RESERVED
No part of this work covered by the copyright hereon may be reproduced or used in any form or by any means—graphic, electronic, or mechanical, including photocopying, recording, taping, Web distribution, or information storage retrieval systems—without the written permission of the publisher.

Articles in Greenhaven Press anthologies are often edited for length to meet page requirements. In addition, original titles of these works are changed to clearly present the main thesis and to explicitly indicate the author's opinion. Every effort is made to ensure that Greenhaven Press accurately reflects the original intent of the authors. Every effort has been made to trace the owners of copyrighted material.

Cover photograph reproduced by permission of © Reuters/CORBIS.

LIBRARY OF CONGRESS CATALOGING-IN-PUBLICATION DATA

The death penalty / Samuel Brenner, book editor
  p. cm. -- (Issues on trial)
  Includes bibliographical references and index. 0-7377-2507-9 (lib. : alk. paper)
  1. Capital punishment--United States--Cases. I. Brenner, Samuel. II. Series.
  KF9227.C2 A52 2006
  345.73'0773--dc22
                                                            2005058851

Printed in the United States of America
10 9 8 7 6 5 4 3 2 1

Contents

Foreward	9
Introduction	12

Chapter 1: Suspending the Death Penalty

Case Overview: *Furman v. Georgia* (1972)   21

The Court's Opinion: The Death Penalty Violates Human Dignity   24
William J. Brennan Jr.

> In one of several concurring opinions in *Furman v. Georgia*, Justice Brennan argues that the death penalty is by its very nature a violation of the prohibition against cruel and unusual punishment and therefore can never be constitutional.

Concurring Opinion: The Death Penalty Is Imposed Arbitrarily   35
Potter Stewart

> Concurring in *Furman v. Georgia*, Justice Potter contends that while the punishment of death may not be unconstitutional in itself, the current application of the penalty in the United States is sufficiently arbitrary to constitute cruel and unusual punishment.

Dissenting Opinion: The Death Penalty Is Constitutional   39
Warren Burger

> Dissenting in *Furman*, Justice Burger maintains that state lawmakers can rewrite their death penalty statutes to conform to the Eighth Amendment.

Creating New Death Penalty Laws After *Furman*   49
Harvard Law Review

> An influential law journal analyzes the *Furman* decision and concludes that in order to make the death penalty constitutional, states need to grant less sentencing discretion to judges and juries.

Chapter 2: Reinstituting and Regulating the Death Penalty

Case Overview: *Gregg v. Georgia* (1976)   **56**

The Court's Opinion: A Properly Directed Death Penalty Is Constitutional   **59**
Potter Stewart

In a plurality opinion in *Gregg v. Georgia*, Justice Stewart concludes that new laws written in the wake of *Furman v. Georgia* ensure that the death penalty is no longer being applied in a cruel and unusual manner and is therefore constitutional.

Dissenting Opinion: The Death Penalty Remains an Excessive Penalty   **70**
Thurgood Marshall

Dissenting in *Gregg*, Justice Marshall insists that the death penalty violates the Eighth Amendment's prohibition of cruel and unusual punishment and fails to achieve the criminal justice goals of deterrence and retribution.

The Death Penalty Is Still Arbitrary   **77**
William Greider

Writing soon after the *Gregg* decision, a journalist argues that the death penalty, even as applied under the new, post-*Furman* statutes, will still constitute cruel and unusual punishment largely because it will be applied in a racist fashion.

The Court Ruled Correctly in *Gregg*   **84**
National Review

A conservative journal celebrates the *Gregg* ruling and argues that it was appropriate for the Court to acknowledge that some crimes are so horrific that states are justified in using capital punishment.

History Shows That *Gregg* Was a Mistake   **87**
Michael L. Radelet

Writing for a group vociferously opposed to capital punishment, a sociology professor argues that the *Gregg* decision represented a serious failure. In the years since the decision the death penalty has been unfairly used against African Americans.

Chapter 3: Forbidding the Execution of the Mentally Retarded

Case Overview: *Atkins v. Virginia* (2002)   **94**

Majority Opinion: Executing the Mentally Retarded Is Excessive Punishment   **97**
John Paul Stevens

In *Atkins v. Virginia* (2002) the Supreme Court ruled that changing standards of morality in American society have led to a national consensus that execution of the mentally retarded is cruel and unusual punishment.

Dissenting Opinion: Executing the Mentally Retarded Is Not Unconstitutional   **105**
Antonin Scalia

In his dissenting opinion in *Atkins*, Justice Scalia insists that no clear national consensus against the execution of the mentally retarded has yet emerged. States should be allowed to decide the issue for themselves.

Atkins Was a Misuse of Psychiatry   **113**
Douglas Mossman

A professor of forensic psychiatry points out serious problems with the Court's ruling in *Atkins* that he says will result in the confused and arbitrary treatment of mental retardation in the future.

Atkins Raises Troubling Moral Questions   **123**
Margaret Talbot

A writer who specializes in cultural politics maintains that the Court's ruling in *Atkins* comes directly into conflict with the prevailing belief in the United States that society should move away from the use of IQ tests.

Atkins Will Destigmatize the Mentally Retarded   **131**
Christopher Slobogin

A law professor maintains that *Atkins* will lead to decreased stigma against the mentally retarded by forcing juries to treat individuals with mental disabilities fairly.

Chapter 4: Forbidding the Execution of Juveniles

Case Overview: *Donald P. Roper, Superintendent, Potosi Correctional Center v. Christopher Simmons* (2005)   **138**

The Court's Opinion: Executing Juveniles   140
    Is Unconstitutional
    Anthony M. Kennedy

    In *Donald P. Roper, Superintendent, Potosi Correctional Center v. Christopher Simmons* (2005), the U.S. Supreme Court points out that the United States was one of only a few nations in the world to allow the execution of juveniles. Furthermore, an emerging national consensus against such executions has rendered the juvenile death penalty cruel and unusual.

Dissenting Opinion: There Is No National   149
    Consensus Against Executing Juveniles
    Sandra Day O'Connor

    Justice O'Connor argues that there is not yet a clear national consensus against juvenile executions and that the majority's decision to use eighteen as the cut-off age for the death penalty is not logical.

Juveniles Are Less Culpable than Adults   159
    The American Bar Association

    An organization of lawyers contends that juveniles are physically and mentally less developed than adults and that it is therefore improper to treat juvenile and adult offenders identically.

Roper Was a Step Toward the Abolition of the   167
    Death Penalty
    The Nation

    The editors of a liberal publication contend that *Roper* added momentum to the movement to ban the death penalty, although the ultimate goal is still far from reality.

The *Roper* Decision Was a Travesty   170
    Robert H. Bork

    A famed legal scholar argues that the *Roper* decision is part of a long-standing effort by the majority of the Court to attack the Constitution and remake the United States.

Organizations to Contact   176
For Further Research   180
Index   185

Foreword

The U.S. courts have long served as a battleground for the most highly charged and contentious issues of the time. Divisive matters are often brought into the legal system by activists who feel strongly for their cause and demand an official resolution. Indeed, subjects that give rise to intense emotions or involve closely held religious or moral beliefs lay at the heart of the most polemical court rulings in history. One such case was *Brown v. Board of Education* (1954), which ended racial segregation in schools. Prior to *Brown*, the courts had held that blacks could be forced to use separate facilities as long as these facilities were equal to that of whites.

For years many groups had opposed segregation based on religious, moral, and legal grounds. Educators produced heartfelt testimony that segregated schooling greatly disadvantaged black children. They noted that in comparison to whites, blacks received a substandard education in deplorable conditions. Religious leaders such as Martin Luther King Jr. preached that the harsh treatment of blacks was immoral and unjust. Many involved in civil rights law, such as Thurgood Marshall, called for equal protection of all people under the law, as their study of the Constitution had indicated that segregation was illegal and un-American. Whatever their motivation for ending the practice, and despite the threats they received from segregationists, these ardent activists remained unwavering in their cause.

Those fighting against the integration of schools were mainly white southerners who did not believe that whites and blacks should intermingle. Blacks were subordinate to whites, they maintained, and society had to resist any attempt to break down strict color lines. Some white southerners charged that segregated schooling was *not* hindering blacks' education. For example, Virginia attorney general J. Lindsay Almond asserted, "With the help and the sympathy and the love and respect of the white people of the South, the colored man has risen under that educational process to a place of eminence and respect throughout the nation. It has served him well." So when the Supreme Court ruled against the segregationists in *Brown*, the South responded with vociferous cries of protest. Even government leaders criticized the decision. The governor of Arkansas, Orval Faubus, stated that he would not "be a party to any attempt to force acceptance of change to which the people are so overwhelmingly opposed." Indeed, resistance to integration was so great that when black students arrived at the formerly all-white Central High School in Arkansas, federal troops had to be dispatched to quell a threatening mob of protesters.

Nevertheless, the *Brown* decision was enforced and the South integrated its schools. In this instance, the Court, while not settling the issue to everyone's satisfaction, functioned as an instrument of progress by forcing a major social change. Historian David Halberstam observes that the *Brown* ruling "deprived segregationist practices of their moral legitimacy.... It was therefore perhaps the single most important moment of the decade, the moment that separated the old order from the new and helped create the tumultuous era just arriving." Considered one of the most important victories for civil rights, *Brown* paved the way for challenges to racial segregation in many areas, including on public buses and in restaurants.

In examining *Brown*, it becomes apparent that the courts play an influential role—and face an arduous challenge—in shaping the debate over emotionally charged social issues. Judges must balance competing interests, keeping in mind the high stakes and intense emotions on both sides. As exemplified by *Brown*, judicial decisions often upset the status quo and initiate significant changes in society. Greenhaven Press's Issues on Trial series captures the controversy surrounding influential court rulings and explores the social ramifications of such decisions from varying perspectives. Each anthology highlights one social issue—such as the death penalty, students' rights, or wartime civil liberties. Each volume then focuses on key historical and contemporary court cases that helped mold the issue as we know it today. The books include a compendium of primary sources—court rulings, dissents, and immediate reactions to the rulings—as well as secondary sources from experts in the field, people involved in the cases, legal analysts, and other commentators opining on the implications and legacy of the chosen cases. An annotated table of contents, an in-depth introduction, and prefaces that overview each case all provide context as readers delve into the topic at hand. To help students fully probe the subject, each volume contains book and periodical bibliographies, a comprehensive index, and a list of organizations to contact. With these features, the Issues on Trial series offers a well-rounded perspective on the courts' role in framing society's thorniest, most impassioned debates.

Introduction

When in 1994 Bruce Callins, a criminal who had been sentenced to death in Texas for the 1980 murder of a bar patron in Fort Worth, appealed his sentence to the U.S. Supreme Court, Justice Harry Blackmun took the opportunity to stake out a clear and final position on capital punishment. Blackmun, who was near the end of his career, had for decades worked to shape and regulate the death penalty—to, as he put it, "develop procedural and substantive rules that would lend more than the mere appearance of fairness to the death penalty endeavor"—but by the time Callins's appeal reached the Court, Blackmun believed his efforts had been pointless. "I feel morally and intellectually obligated simply to concede that the death penalty experiment has failed," Blackmun declared. "From this day forward, I no longer shall tinker with the machinery of death."[1] Blackmun's colleague, Justice Antonin Scalia, responded to Blackmun's unusually emotional opinion by pointing out that the Supreme Court needed to base its opinions on laws rather than feelings. "Convictions in opposition to the death penalty are often passionate and deeply held," Scalia noted. "That would be no excuse for reading them into a Constitution that does not contain them."[2] Ultimately, the Supreme Court refused to hear Callins's appeal; Callins was executed by lethal injection on May 21, 1997.

In *Callins* both Blackmun and Scalia were speaking to one of the most divisive issues in American jurisprudence: whether it is appropriate for the state to tie a criminal to an electric chair, place a noose around his neck, insert a poison-carrying needle into his arm, or lock him into a gas chamber, and then to kill him as punishment for a crime for which he has been found guilty. Given the Supreme Court's unique role as the final arbiter of what legislation is prohibited by the Constitution, and given that the members of the Court are human, with human concerns and human ideals, Supreme Court death penalty cases have routinely swung between emotion and law, prejudice and analysis. The history of modern death penalty jurisprudence is the history of a nation, a society, and a judiciary struggling to ensure that, while criminals are punished for their crimes, the nation remains true to its values and its laws and treats convicts fairly.

Any discussion of modern death penalty jurisprudence must necessarily begin with *Furman v. Georgia* (1972), which, as noted in the 1995 *Harvard Law Review*, "easily wins as *the* landmark Supreme Court decision regarding capital punishment."[3] In 1972 the Supreme Court stunned the nation when it ruled by 5-4 in *Furman* that the death penalty, as it then existed in the United States, violated the Eighth Amendment prohibition against "cruel and unusual" punishment because of its arbitrary and possibly even discriminatory application. In one of the most memorable phrases to come from the opinion, Justice Potter Stewart—himself no knee-jerk opponent of capital punishment—observed that the death sentences under review "are cruel and unusual in the same way that being struck by lightning is cruel and unusual." Given that there were no clear guidelines governing the imposition of the death penalty, and given that only a handful of those convicted of serious crimes had been sentenced to death, Stewart argued that the death penalty was being applied "wantonly and ... freakishly."[4] The issue of capital punishment was so clearly important to the justices that in *Furman* each of them wrote a separate opinion to explain his personal thinking.

While the ruling itself came as a shock, *Furman* changed very little on the ground because executions had actually been halted unofficially in the United States several years before in response to general unease over problems with how the death penalty was administered. What *Furman* did was force state and federal legislators to craft new death penalty statutes and usher in decades of debate over when it is permissible for the state to sentence someone to die. Two sorts of new death penalty statutes emerged after *Furman*: the first provided for "guided discretion," under which juries, having already found offenders guilty in earlier phases of trials and after hearing mitigating and aggravating evidence, were allowed to decide when to sentence offenders to death. The second type of law provided for mandatory death sentences in cases of specific crimes. Guided discretion statutes were upheld by the Supreme Court in three related cases: *Gregg v. Georgia* (1976), *Jurek v. Texas* (1976), and *Proffitt v. Florida* (1976). The mandatory death penalty laws, which allowed judges and juries no discretion beyond the determination of guilt, were meanwhile found unconstitutional in *Woodson v. North Carolina* (1976) and *Roberts v. Louisiana* (1976). All death penalty legislation and jurisprudence since 1976 has built on the guidelines approved of and laid out in *Gregg*.

With its 7-2 decision in *Gregg v. Georgia* (*Gregg, Jurek*, and *Proffitt*, the three guided discretion cases, were bundled together and heard as a single unit) the Supreme Court signaled its belief that capital punishment could be constitutional as long as the death penalty was serving a criminal justice purpose (such as deterring crime) and was being applied evenhandedly, in a nonarbitrary fashion. Despite this decision, however, the Court was not indicating blanket approval of the way death penalty cases were being handled. Over the next few years the Court handed down a number of decisions that limited and refined the use of capital punishment with the goal of (as Blackmun later stated) making the death penalty truly fair. In *Coker v. Georgia* (1977), for instance, the Court held that the death penalty for the rape of adult women was unconstitutional because the sentence was disproportionate to the crime. In *Lockett v. Ohio* (1978) the Court ruled that judges and juries must be able to consider all possible mitigating evidence, whether or not it was relevant to the crime. In

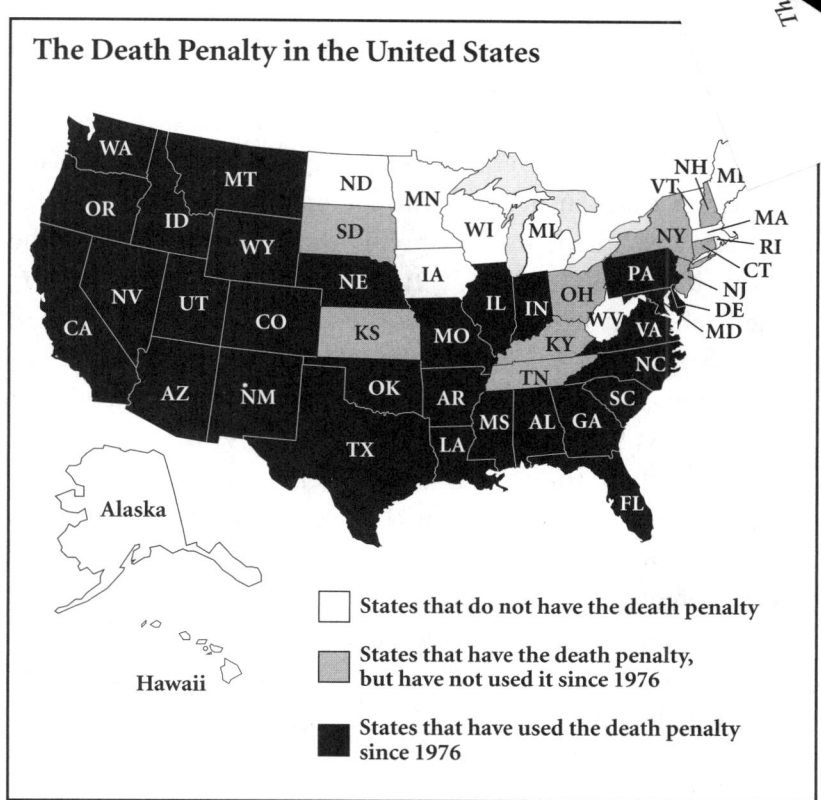

Godfrey v. Georgia (1980) the Court signaled again its concern that the death penalty be applied in a clear and consistent manner and that juries be carefully guided when imposing the death penalty. In that case the court ruled that a death sentence must be based on more than a finding that the offense was "outrageously or wantonly vile, horrible, or inhumane." Judging that all murders meet that description, the justices concluded that juries that wanted to sentence an offender to death could use that statutory aggravating circumstance at will, and that the balance ensured by "guided discretion" would thus be threatened.

In 1986, with its ruling in *Ford v. Wainwright*, the Supreme Court began to address a new question: whether some classes of offenders such as the insane, juveniles, the mentally retarded, or even racial minorities should be altogether exempt from the death penalty. In *Ford v. Wainwright* the Court held that it was unconstitutional to execute an insane offender, ruling that "it is no less abhorrent today than it has been for centuries to exact in penance the life of one whose mental illness prevents him from comprehending the reasons for the penalty or its implications."[5] In general, however, the Court seemed reluctant to disqualify entire classes of offenders from the death penalty. In *Thompson v. Oklahoma* (1988) and *Stanford v. Kentucky* (1989), for instance, the Court concluded that it was permissible to execute offenders who were over the age of sixteen when they committed their crimes. In *Penry v. Lynaugh* (1989) the Court similarly concluded that there was no constitutional prohibition against execution of the mentally retarded.

In the late 1990s and early 2000s the Court substantially changed direction in its capital punishment decisions, largely as a result of the increasing liberalism of Justice Anthony Kennedy, who had been appointed by President Ronald Reagan, and the addition to the Court of Justices Ruth Bader Ginsburg and Stephen Breyer, both of whom were appointed by President William Clinton. Perhaps the two most important modern cases were *Atkins v. Virginia* (2002) and *Roper v. Simmons* (2005). In *Atkins* the Court ruled that the mentally retarded bear diminished culpability for their crimes and that "evolving standards of decency" have rendered execution of the mentally retarded unconstitutional. Taking this argument to its logical conclusion, in *Roper* the justices (four of whom had earlier issued a statement characterizing execution of juvenile killers as "shameful") ruled that both because of evolving national standards and because juveniles are less fully developed than adults, juveniles under eighteen are immune from execution as well. During the same period, in *Rompilla v. Beard* (2005), the Court also reaffirmed its requirement that offenders threatened with the death penalty must have adequate representation.

These cases represent only a few of the many death penalty cases decided by the Supreme Court, but they both help identify a vague pattern to the Supreme Court's rulings and indicate how close decisions about capital punishment are in the United States. While the Supreme Court's death penalty decisions since *Furman* have not yet resulted in a clear and understandable capital punishment system, they do seem to be leading in a clear direction: The death penalty, the justices seem to be saying, is acceptable and constitutional in contemporary American society when state and federal legislators wish it to be acceptable, when it is imposed in an evenhanded, fair, and nonarbitrary fashion, and when those sentenced to death truly bear full responsibility and culpability for their actions. In other words, the majority of the justices seem to want to preserve the death penalty as an institution while increasingly restricting and paring down the ways in which states can use it to put offenders to death.

The piecemeal manner in which the death penalty is being restricted is somewhat confusing. As Scalia, one of the most vocal and effective opponents of the Court's new direction in death penalty jurisprudence, noted in his biting dissent in *Atkins*, "There is something to be said for popular abolition of the death penalty; there is nothing to be said for its incremental abolition by this Court."[6] Scalia was objecting not only to the piecemeal nature of these restrictions on the death penalty but also to the fact that (in his opinion) the majority of the justices seem to be ruling more on the basis of emotion than on the basis of rigorous logic and constitutional law. Scalia's objections appear to be based in his belief that death penalty decisions are properly the purview of the legislatures rather than the courts and in his disgust for what he sees as poor logic on the part of the majority. Reading his dissent in *Roper* from the bench, for instance, Scalia dismissed the majority's actions as "no way to run a legal system" and suggested that the Court's modern death penalty decisions essentially constitute "a show of hands on the current Justices' personal views."[7] Scalia's concerns have been echoed both by Chief Justice William Rehnquist (who has added his own criticisms of how the majority of justices, in identifying "evolving national standards," are citing popular opinion data and even foreign laws) and by Justice Clarence Thomas. Even centrist Justice Sandra Day O'Connor shares some of Scalia's concerns. Just before announcing her retirement in 2005, for example, O'Connor wrote a key dissent in *Roper* arguing that the "emerging national consensus" the majority of the Court had found against the execution of juvenile killers simply did not exist.

While Scalia and Thomas (who will likely be joined in their opinions by Chief Justice John Roberts and Justice Samuel Alito, both of whom were appointed to the Court by President George W. Bush) are for the moment outnumbered in these cases restricting use of the death penalty, it seems clear that their comments are not necessarily those of a defeated minority. Given that many of the most important death penalty cases in the late 1990s and early 2000s, including both *Atkins* and *Roper*, were decided by 5-4 margins, and that others were decided by 6-3 margins, a shift by one or two justices could have a radical effect on the manner in which the death penalty is administered in the United States. While Blackmun was ready to declare in 1994 that he would "no longer tinker with the machinery of death," the serving justices seem dedicated to "tinkering" with death penalty statutes so as to ensure a fair and reasonable system of justice. It is clear, then, that the Court, along with American society, continues to struggle with the difficult questions raised by the death penalty.

Notes

1. Harry Blackmun, dissenting opinion, *Callins v. Collins*, 510 U.S. 1141.
2. Antonin Scalia, concurring opinion, *Callins v. Collins*, 510 U.S. 1141.
3. Carol S. Steiker and Jordan M. Steiker, "Sober Second Thoughts: Reflections on Two Decades of Constitutional Regulation of Capital Punishment," *Harvard Law*

Review, vol. 109, no. 2, December 1995, p. 362.
4. Potter Stewart, concurring opinion, *Furman v. Georgia*, 408 U.S. 238.
5. Thurgood Marshall, majority opinion, *Ford v. Wainwright*, 477 U.S. 399.
6. Antonin Scalia, dissenting opinion, *Atkins v. Virginia*, 536 U.S. 304.
7. Antonin Scalia, dissenting opinion, *Donald P. Roper, Superintendent, Potosi Correctional Center v. Christopher Simmons*, 543 U.S.

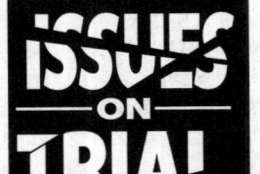

CHAPTER 1

Suspending the Death Penalty

Chapter Preface

Case Overview: *Furman v. Georgia* (1972)

In *Furman v. Georgia* the United States Supreme Court ruled 5-4 that the death penalty, as then applied in the United States, amounted to "cruel and unusual" punishment and therefore violated the Eighth and Fourteenth Amendments. The Court actually reviewed three cases, which it bundled together under one ruling. One of these cases was that of William Furman, a small-time thief in Georgia who had been in the process of burglarizing a family home when he was interrupted by one of the residents. While trying to escape, Furman apparently tripped, accidentally fired his gun, and killed a member of the family that lived in the house. Furman was arrested, tried, convicted of murder, and sentenced to death. At the time, juries in Georgia were given wide discretion in applying the death penalty; if they believed that the crime in question had been particularly heinous, then they could at will sentence the offender to death. Furman and his lawyers appealed the death sentence, arguing that by giving such wide discretion to juries, Georgia's laws resulted in the arbitrary application of the death penalty.

The Court's per curiam (by the court) decision in *Furman* was only one paragraph long and was relatively straightforward, noting simply that the death penalty in these cases was unconstitutional. As a whole, however, the *Furman* ruling proved relatively complex, and in an unusual move each of the nine justices wrote a separate opinion, generating in total over two hundred pages of material. On one extreme of the five-justice majority were Justices William Brennan and Thurgood Marshall, who argued respectively that capital punishment did not "comport with human dignity" and that in all cases the death penalty was morally unacceptable to the people of the United States. Justices William O. Douglas, Potter Stewart, and Byron R. White were less willing to state categorical opposition to capital punishment, instead noting that the death penalty *as it then existed* was being applied freakishly and capriciously, especially in the case of minority defendants. If the laws were changed to eliminate the arbitrary nature of the death penalty, they implied, capital punishment might once again become acceptable.

The four dissenting justices, meanwhile, generally agreed that the Court (and, by extension, the judicial branch of the government) had no right to interfere in what was more properly the bailiwick of the legislative branch and the state governments. Chief Justice Warren Burger and Justices Harry Blackmun, Lewis F. Powell, and William H. Rehnquist argued that judges have a responsibility to exercise judicial self-restraint and that the Court should not use the Eighth Amendment to seize power from the legislatures.

Because of the complexity of the nine opinions, the *Furman* ruling engendered some confusion among the state and federal legislatures over exactly what the Court had decided. It was clear that a slim majority of the Court had ruled that the sentences of death should be overturned for the offenders in the three cases bundled into *Furman* (and, by extension, for all those sentenced to death in the United States), but it remained unclear whether the Court had decided that capital punishment would *always* be unacceptable and unconstitutional. Those seeking to reinstate the death penalty—including the majority of legislators in over half of the states as well as all those in the Nixon administration—found some guidance in Burger's dissent. The chief justice had suggested that the legislatures could designate particular crimes, such as the killing of police officers, as crimes worthy of the death penalty. They received additional guidance from Stewart, who seemed uncomfortable with the thought of reaching a permanent conclusion about capital punishment and who implied that legislatures needed to eliminate the capricious, discriminatory, and arbitrary manner in which the death penalty was being applied. The *Furman* ruling thus ushered in a period during which death penalty advocates worked to redesign and structure criminal statutes so as to create clear, logical, and fair guidelines for determining when offenders should be sentenced to die.

| "Death is today a 'cruel and unusual' punishment."

The Court's Opinion: The Death Penalty Violates Human Dignity

William J. Brennan Jr.

In his concurring opinion in Furman v. Georgia *(1972), excerpted here, Justice William J. Brennan Jr. argued that the death penalty as then applied in the United States violated the Eighth and Fourteenth Amendments because it constituted "cruel and unusual" punishment. Acknowledging that the phrase "cruel and unusual" had never been adequately and fully defined, Brennan suggested that punishments must "comport with human dignity" and accordingly must be judged on four principles: whether they are degrading to human dignity, are applied arbitrarily by the state, are unacceptable to contemporary society, or are excessive given the crimes. Brennan concluded that the punishment of death was unusually degrading, that it was probably being applied in an arbitrary fashion, that its rejection by contemporary society was "virtually total," and that it served no function that could not be equally well-served by life imprisonment. As such, Brennan argued, the punishment of death did not comport with human dignity and was therefore unconstitutional. Brennan served as an associate justice on the Court from 1957 until his retirement in 1990.*

The question presented in these cases is whether death is today a punishment for crime that is "cruel and unusual"

William J. Brennan Jr., concurring opinion, *Furman v. Georgia*, U.S. Supreme Court, June 29, 1972.

and consequently, by virtue of the Eighth and Fourteenth Amendments, beyond the power of the State to inflict.

Almost a century ago, this Court observed that

> [d]ifficulty would attend the effort to define with exactness the extent of the constitutional provision which provides that cruel and unusual punishments shall not be inflicted. *Wilkerson v. Utah* (1879).

Less than 15 years ago, it was again noted that "[t]he exact scope of the constitutional phrase 'cruel and unusual' has not been detailed by this Court." *Trop v. Dulles* (1958). Those statements remain true today. The Cruel and Unusual Punishments Clause, like the other great clauses of the Constitution, is not susceptible of precise definition. Yet we know that the values and ideals it embodies are basic to our scheme of government. And we know also that the Clause imposes upon this Court the duty, when the issue is properly presented, to determine the constitutional validity of a challenged punishment, whatever that punishment may be. In these cases, "[t]hat issue confronts us, and the task of resolving it is inescapably ours." [*Trop v. Dulles.*] . . .

Protecting the Dignity of Man

At bottom, then, the Cruel and Unusual Punishments Clause prohibits the infliction of uncivilized and inhuman punishments. The State, even as it punishes, must treat its members with respect for their intrinsic worth as human beings. A punishment is "cruel and unusual," therefore, if it does not comport with human dignity.

This formulation, of course, does not, of itself, yield principles for assessing the constitutional validity of particular punishments. Nevertheless, even though "[t]his Court has had little occasion to give precise content to the [Clause]," [*Trop v. Dulles*], there are principles recognized in our cases and inherent in the Clause sufficient to permit a judicial determina tion whether a challenged punishment comports with human dignity.

The primary principle is that a punishment must not be so severe as to be degrading to the dignity of human beings. Pain, certainly, may be a factor in the judgment. The infliction of an extremely severe punishment will often entail physical suffering.

Yet the Framers also knew "that there could be exercises of cruelty by laws other than those which inflicted bodily pain or mutilation." [*Weems v. United States* (1910)] Even though "[t]here may be involved no physical mistreatment, no primitive torture," *Trop v. Dulles*, severe mental pain may be inherent in the infliction of a particular punishment. That, indeed, was one of the conclusions underlying the holding of the plurality in *Trop v. Dulles* that the punishment of expatriation violates the Clause. And the physical and mental suffering inherent in the punishment of *cadena temporal* [twelve years in chains at hard labor], was an obvious basis for the Court's decision in *Weems v. United States* that the punishment was "cruel and unusual."

More than the presence of pain, however, is comprehended in the judgment that the extreme severity of a punishment makes it degrading to the dignity of human beings. The barbaric punishments condemned by history, "punishments which inflict torture, such as the rack, the thumbscrew, the iron boot, the stretching of limbs and the like," are, of course, "attended with acute pain and suffering." *O'Neil v. Vermont* (1892). ([Stephen] Field, J., dissenting). When we consider why they have been condemned, however, we realize that the pain involved is not the only reason. The true significance of these punishments is that they treat members of the human race as nonhumans, as objects to be toyed with and discarded. They are thus inconsistent with the fundamental premise of the Clause that even the vilest criminal remains a human being possessed of common human dignity....

Rejecting Arbitrary and Unacceptable Punishment

In determining whether a punishment comports with human dignity, we are aided also by a second principle inherent in the Clause—that the State must not arbitrarily inflict a severe punishment. This principle derives from the notion that the State does not respect human dignity when, without reason, it inflicts upon some people a severe punishment that it does not inflict upon others. Indeed, the very words "cruel and unusual punishments" imply condemnation of the arbitrary infliction of severe punishments. And, as we now know, the English history of the Clause reveals a particular concern with the establishment of a safeguard against arbitrary punishments. . . .

A third principle inherent in the Clause is that a severe punishment must not be unacceptable to contemporary society. Rejection by society, of course, is a strong indication that a severe punishment does not comport with human dignity. In applying this principle, however, we must make certain that the judicial determination is as objective as possible. Thus, for example, *Weems v. United States* and *Trop v. Dulles* suggest that one factor that may be considered is the existence of the punishment in jurisdictions other than those before the Court. *Wilkerson v. Utah* suggests that another factor to be considered is the historic usage of the punishment. *Trop v. Dulles* combined present acceptance with past usage by observing that

> the death penalty has been employed throughout our history, and, in a day when it is still widely accepted, it cannot be said to violate the constitutional concept of cruelty.

In *Robinson v. California* [1962], which involved the infliction of punishment for narcotics addiction, the Court went a step further, concluding simply that,

The Death Penalty

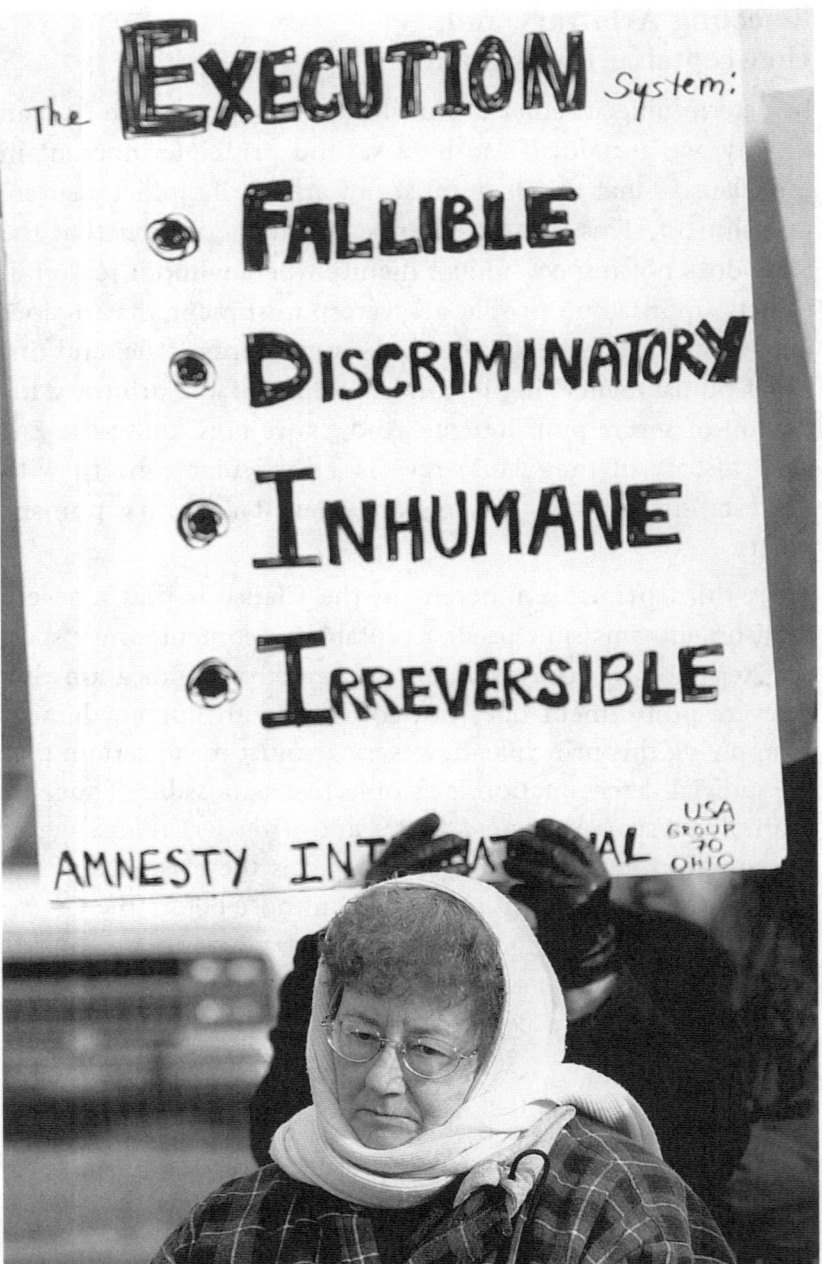

Justice Brennan's arguments reflect the beliefs of those opposed to the death penalty. Getty Images

in the light of contemporary human knowledge, a law which made a criminal offense of such a disease would doubtless be universally thought to be an infliction of cruel and unusual punishment.

The question under this principle, then, is whether there are objective indicators from which a court can conclude that contemporary society considers a severe punishment unacceptable. Accordingly, the judicial task is to review the history of a challenged punishment and to examine society's present practices with respect to its use. Legislative authorization, of course, does not establish acceptance. The acceptability of a severe punishment is measured not by its availability, for it might become so offensive to society as never to be inflicted, but by its use.

The final principle inherent in the Clause is that a severe punishment must not be excessive. A punishment is excessive under this principle if it is unnecessary: the infliction of a severe punishment by the State cannot comport with human dignity when it is nothing more than the pointless infliction of suffering. If there is a significantly less severe punishment adequate to achieve the purposes for which the punishment is inflicted, the punishment inflicted is unnecessary, and therefore excessive. . . .

Judging Punishments "Cruel and Unusual"

There are, then, four principles by which we may determine whether a particular punishment is "cruel and unusual." The primary principle, which I believe supplies the essential predicate for the application of the others, is that a punishment must not, by its severity, be degrading to human dignity. The paradigm violation of this principle would be the infliction of a torturous punishment of the type that the Clause has always prohibited. Yet "[i]t is unlikely that any State at this moment in history," *Robinson v. California*, would pass a law providing for the infliction of such a punishment. Indeed, no such punishment has ever been before this Court. The same may be said of the other principles. It is unlikely that this Court will confront a severe punishment that is obviously inflicted in wholly arbitrary fashion; no State would engage in a reign of blind terror. Nor is it likely that this Court will be called upon to review a severe punishment that is clearly and totally rejected throughout society; no legislature would be able even to authorize the infliction of such a punishment. Nor, finally, is it likely that this Court will have to consider a severe punishment that is patently unnecessary; no State today would inflict a severe punishment knowing that there was no reason whatever for doing so. In short, we are unlikely to have occasion to determine that a punishment is fatally offensive under any one principle.

Since the Bill of Rights was adopted, this Court has adjudged only three punishments to be within the prohibition of the Clause. See *Weems v. United States* (1910) (12 years in chains at hard and painful labor); *Trop v. Dulles* (1958) (expatriation); *Robinson v. California* (1962) (imprisonment for narcotics addiction). Each punishment, of course, was degrading to human dignity, but of none could it be said conclusively that it was fatally offensive under one or the other of the principles. Rather, these "cruel and unusual punishments" seriously implicated several of the principles, and it was the application of the principles in combination that supported the judgment. That, indeed, is not surprising. The function of these principles, after all, is simply to provide means by which a court can determine whether a challenged punishment comports with human dignity. They are, therefore, interrelated, and, in most cases, it will be their convergence that will justify the conclusion that a punishment is "cruel and unusual." The test, then, will ordinarily be a cumulative one: if a punishment is unusually severe, if there is a strong probability that it is inflicted arbitrarily, if it is substantially rejected by contemporary society, and if there is no reason to believe that it serves any penal purpose more effectively than some less severe punishment, then the continued infliction of that punishment violates the command of the Clause that the State may not inflict inhuman and uncivilized punishments upon those convicted of crimes.

Death Is "Cruel and Unusual" Punishment

The punishment challenged in these cases is death. Death, of course, is a "traditional" punishment, *Trop v. Dulles*, one that "has been employed throughout our history." . . .

The question, then, is whether the deliberate infliction of death is today consistent with the command of the Clause that the State may not inflict punishments that do not comport with human dignity. I will analyze the punishment of death in terms of the principles set out above and the cumulative test to which they lead: it is a denial of human dignity for the State arbitrarily to subject a person to an unusually severe punishment that society has indicated it does not regard as acceptable, and that cannot be shown to serve any penal purpose more effectively than a significantly less drastic punishment. Under these principles and this test, death is today a "cruel and unusual" punishment. Death is a unique punishment in the United States. In a society that so strongly affirms the sanctity of life, not surprisingly, the common view is that death is the ultimate sanction. This natural human feeling appears all about us. There has been no national debate about punishment in general, or by imprisonment, comparable to the debate about the punishment of death. No other punishment has been so continuously restricted, nor has any State yet abolished prisons, as some have abolished this punishment. And those States that still inflict death reserve it for the most heinous crimes. Juries, of course, have always treated death cases differently, as have governors exercising their commutation powers. Criminal defendants are of the same views.

The only explanation for the uniqueness of death is its extreme severity. Death is today an unusually severe punishment, unusual in its pain, in its finality, and in its enormity. No other existing punishment is comparable to death in terms of physical and mental suffering. Although our information is not conclusive, it appears that there is no method available that guarantees an immediate and painless death. Since the discontinuance of flogging as a constitutionally permissible punishment, death remains as the only punishment that may involve the conscious infliction of physical pain. In addition, we know that mental pain is an inseparable part of our practice of punishing criminals by death, for the prospect of pending execution exacts a frightful toll during the inevitable long wait between the imposition of sentence and the actual infliction of death. As the California Supreme Court pointed out, "the process of carrying out a verdict of death is often so degrading and brutalizing to the human spirit as to constitute psychological torture." *People v. Anderson* (1972). Indeed, as Mr. Justice [Felix] Frankfurter noted, "the onset of insanity while awaiting execution of a death sentence is not a rare phenomenon." *Solesbee v. Balkcom* (1950) (dissenting opinion). The "fate of ever-increasing fear and distress" to which the expatriate is subjected, *Trop v. Dulles*, can only exist to a greater degree for a person confined in prison awaiting death. . . .

Death Is Awesome and Degrading

Death is truly an awesome punishment. The calculated killing of a human being by the State involves, by its very nature, a denial of the executed person's humanity. The contrast with the plight of a person punished by imprisonment is evident. An individual in prison does not lose "the right to have rights." A prisoner retains, for example, the constitutional rights to the free exercise of religion, to be free of cruel and unusual punishments, and to treatment as a "person" for purposes of due process of law and the equal protection of the laws. A prisoner remains a member of the human family. Moreover, he retains the right of access to the courts. His punishment is not irrevocable. Apart from the common charge, grounded upon the recognition of human fallibility, that the punishment of death must inevitably be inflicted upon innocent men, we know that death has been the lot of men whose convictions were unconstitutionally secured in view of later, retroactively applied, holdings of this Court. . . .

An Arbitrarily Inflicted Punishment

In comparison to all other punishments today, then, the deliberate extinguishment of human life by the State is uniquely degrading to human dignity. I would not hesitate to hold, on that ground alone, that death is today a "cruel and unusual" punishment, were it not that death is a punishment of longstanding usage and acceptance in this country. I therefore turn to the second principle—that the State may not arbitrarily inflict an unusually severe punishment.

The outstanding characteristic of our present practice of punishing criminals by death is the infrequency with which we resort to it. The evidence is conclusive that death is not the ordinary punishment for any crime. . . .

When a country of over 200 million people inflicts an unusually severe punishment no more than 50 times a year, the inference is strong that the punishment is not being regularly and fairly applied. To dispel it would indeed require a clear showing of nonarbitrary infliction.

Although there are no exact figures available, we know that thousands of murders and rapes are committed annually in States where death is an authorized punishment for those crimes. However the rate of infliction is characterized—as "freakishly" or "spectacularly" rare, or simply as rare—it would take the purest sophistry to deny that death is inflicted in only a minute fraction of these cases. How much rarer, after all, could the infliction of death be?

When the punishment of death is inflicted in a trivial number of the cases in which it is legally available, the conclusion is virtually inescapable that it is being inflicted arbitrarily. Indeed, it smacks of little more than a lottery system. . . .

When there is a strong probability that an unusually severe and degrading punishment is being inflicted arbitrarily, we may well expect that society will disapprove of its infliction. I turn, therefore, to the third principle. An examination of the history and present operation of the American practice of punishing criminals by death reveals that this punishment has been almost totally rejected by contemporary society. . . .

The final principle to be considered is that an unusually severe and degrading punishment may not be excessive in view of the purposes for which it is inflicted. This principle, too, is related to the others. When there is a strong probability that the State is arbitrarily inflicting an unusually severe punishment that is subject to grave societal doubts, it is likely also that the punishment cannot be shown to be serving any penal purpose that could not be served equally well by some less severe punishment. . . .

In sum, the punishment of death is inconsistent with all four principles: death is an unusually severe and degrading punishment; there is a strong probability that it is inflicted arbitrarily; its rejection by contemporary society is virtually total; and there is no reason to believe that it serves any penal purpose more effectively than the less severe punishment of imprisonment. The function of these principles is to enable a court to determine whether a punishment comports with human dignity. Death, quite simply, does not.

> "These death sentences are cruel and unusual in the same way that being struck by lightning is cruel and unusual."

Concurring Opinion: The Death Penalty Is Imposed Arbitrarily

Potter Stewart

In his concurring opinion in Furman v. Georgia, *Justice Potter Stewart argued that the death penalty, as it was then being applied in the United States, violated the Eighth and Fourteenth Amendments. Stewart believed that the death penalty was cruel and unusual primarily in that it was imposed arbitrarily, noting that whether criminals were sentenced to death was as random as whether individuals were struck by lightning. The result, Stewart concluded, was that the death penalty was being applied "wantonly and freakishly." Stewart, however, refused to consider whether the death penalty was unconstitutional in all cases and left open the possibility that he might reconsider his opinion. Indeed, Stewart added that he saw value in the death penalty as an instrument of retribution, which he said was "part of the nature of man." When in 1976 the Supreme Court reversed its decision in* Furman *by ruling in* Gregg v. Georgia *that the death penalty could be applied constitutionally if the legislatures provided appropriate sentencing guidelines for juries, it was Justice Stewart himself who wrote the majority opinion. Stewart was nominated to the Supreme Court by President Dwight D. Eisen-*

Potter Stewart, concurring opinion, *Furman v. Georgia*, U.S. Supreme Court, June 29, 1972.

hower in October 1958 and served as an associate justice until his retirement in 1981.

The penalty of death differs from all other forms of criminal punishment, not in degree, but in kind. It is unique in its total irrevocability. It is unique in its rejection of rehabilitation of the convict as a basic purpose of criminal justice. And it is unique, finally, in its absolute renunciation of all that is embodied in our concept of humanity.

For these and other reasons, at least two of my Brothers have concluded that the infliction of the death penalty is constitutionally impermissible in all circumstances under the Eighth and Fourteenth Amendments. Their case is a strong one. But I find it unnecessary to reach the ultimate question they would decide.

The opinions of other Justices today have set out in admirable and thorough detail the origins and judicial history of the Eighth Amendment's guarantee against the infliction of cruel and unusual punishments, and the origin and judicial history of capital punishment. There is thus no need for me to review the historical materials here, and what I have to say can, therefore, be briefly stated. Legislatures—state and federal—have sometimes specified that the penalty of death shall be the mandatory punishment for every person convicted of engaging in certain designated criminal conduct. Congress, for example, has provided that anyone convicted of acting as a spy for the enemy in time of war shall be put to death. The Rhode Island Legislature has ordained the death penalty for a life term prisoner who commits murder. Massachusetts has passed a law imposing the death penalty upon anyone convicted of murder in the commission of a forcible rape. An Ohio law imposes the mandatory penalty of death upon the assassin of the President of the United States or the Governor of a State.

No Need to Judge All Capital Punishment

If we were reviewing death sentences imposed under these or similar laws, we would be faced with the need to decide whether capital punishment is unconstitutional for all crimes and under all circumstances. We would need to decide whether a legislature—state or federal—could constitutionally determine that certain criminal conduct is so atrocious that society's interest in deterrence and retribution wholly outweighs any considerations of reform or rehabilitation of the perpetrator, and that, despite the inconclusive empirical evidence, only the automatic penalty of death will provide maximum deterrence.

On that score I would say only that I cannot agree that retribution is a constitutionally impermissible ingredient in the imposition of punishment. The instinct for retribution is part of the nature of man, and channeling that instinct in the administration of criminal justice serves an important purpose in promoting the stability of a society governed by law. When people begin to believe that organized society is unwilling or unable to impose upon criminal offenders the punishment they "deserve," then there are sown the seeds of anarchy—of self-help, vigilante justice, and lynch law.

The constitutionality of capital punishment in the abstract is not, however, before us in these cases. For the Georgia and Texas Legislatures have not provided that the death penalty shall be imposed upon all those who are found guilty of forcible rape. And the Georgia Legislature has not ordained that death shall be the automatic punishment for murder. In a word, neither State has made a legislative determination that forcible rape and murder can be deterred only by imposing the penalty of death upon all who perpetrate those offenses. As Mr. Justice [Byron] White so tellingly puts it, the "legislative will is not frustrated if the penalty is never imposed."

The Death Penalty Is Currently Arbitrary

Instead, the death sentences now before us are the product of a legal system that brings them, I believe, within the very core of the Eighth Amendment's guarantee against cruel and unusual punishments, a guarantee applicable against the States through the Fourteenth Amendment. In the first place, it is clear that these sentences are "cruel" in the sense that they excessively go beyond, not in degree but in kind, the punishments that the state legislatures have determined to be necessary. In the second place, it is equally clear that these sentences are "unusual" in the sense that the penalty of death is infrequently imposed for murder, and that its imposition for rape is extraordinarily rare. But I do not rest my conclusion upon these two propositions alone.

These death sentences are cruel and unusual in the same way that being struck by lightning is cruel and unusual. For, of all the people convicted of rapes and murders in 1967 and 1968, many just as reprehensible as these, the petitioners are among a capriciously selected random handful upon whom the sentence of death has in fact been imposed. My concurring Brothers have demonstrated that, if any basis can be discerned for the selection of these few to be sentenced to die, it is the constitutionally impermissible basis of race. But racial discrimination has not been proved, and I put it to one side. I simply conclude that the Eighth and Fourteenth Amendments cannot tolerate the infliction of a sentence of death under legal systems that permit this unique penalty to be so wantonly and so freakishly imposed.

For these reasons I concur in the judgments of the Court.

> "The constitutional prohibition against 'cruel and unusual punishments' cannot be construed to bar the imposition of the punishment of death."

Dissenting Opinion: The Death Penalty Is Constitutional

Warren Burger

In this dissent to Furman v. Georgia, *Chief Justice Warren Burger concluded that the death penalty did not violate the Eighth and Fourteenth Amendments. Burger added that while a majority of the justices found the death penalty arbitrary and unconstitutional as it was then being applied, and while he personally disapproved of capital punishment, only two justices—a small minority of the Court—had concluded that the death penalty was inherently unconstitutional. Therefore, he concluded, it was now up to the state and federal legislatures to craft new statutes that would render administration of the death penalty less arbitrary and more likely to meet with approval from the majority of the justices. Burger was joined in this dissent by Justices Harry Blackmun, Lewis F. Powell Jr., and William Rehnquist. Burger served as chief justice of the United States Supreme Court from 1969 to 1985.*

At the outset, it is important to note that only two members of the Court, Mr. Justice [William J.] Brennan and Mr. Justice [Thurgood] Marshall, have concluded that the

Warren Burger, dissenting opinion, *Furman v. Georgia*, U.S. Supreme Court, June 29, 1972.

Eighth Amendment prohibits capital punishment for all crimes and under all circumstances. Mr. Justice [William] Douglas has also determined that the death penalty contravenes the Eighth Amendment, although I do not read his opinion as necessarily requiring final abolition of the penalty.... I conclude that the constitutional prohibition against "cruel and unusual punishments" cannot be construed to bar the imposition of the punishment of death.

Mr. Justice [Potter] Stewart and Mr. Justice [Byron] White have concluded that petitioners' death sentences must be set aside because prevailing sentencing practices do not comply with the Eighth Amendment.... I believe this approach fundamentally misconceives the nature of the Eighth Amendment guarantee and flies directly in the face of controlling authority of extremely recent vintage.

Defining "Cruel" and "Unusual"

If we were possessed of legislative power, I would either join with Mr. Justice Brennan and Mr. Justice Marshall or, at the very least, restrict the use of capital punishment to a small category of the most heinous crimes. Our constitutional inquiry, however, must be divorced from personal feelings as to the morality and efficacy of the death penalty, and be confined to the meaning and applicability of the uncertain language of the Eighth Amendment. There is no novelty in being called upon to interpret a constitutional provision that is less than self-defining, but, of all our fundamental guarantees, the ban on "cruel and unusual punishments" is one of the most difficult to translate into judicially manageable terms. The widely divergent views of the Amendment expressed in today's opinions reveal the haze that surrounds this constitutional command. Yet it is essential to our role as a court that we not seize upon the enigmatic character of the guarantee as an invitation to enact our personal predilections into law.

Although the Eighth Amendment literally reads as prohibiting only those punishments that are both "cruel" and "unusual," history compels the conclusion that the Constitution prohibits all punishments of extreme and barbarous cruelty, regardless of how frequently or infrequently imposed. . . .

The Death Penalty Has a Long History in America

It is only 14 years since Mr. Chief Justice [Earl] Warren, speaking for four members of the Court, stated without equivocation:

> Whatever the arguments may be against capital punishment, both on moral grounds and in terms of accomplishing the purposes of punishment—and they are forceful—the death penalty has been employed throughout our history, and, in a day when it is still widely accepted, it cannot be said to violate the constitutional concept of cruelty. [*Trop v. Dulles* (1958).]

It is only one year since Mr. Justice Black made his feelings clear on the constitutional issue:

> The Eighth Amendment forbids "cruel and unusual punishments." In my view, these words cannot be read to outlaw capital punishment, because that penalty was in common use and authorized by law here and in the countries from which our ancestors came at the time the Amendment was adopted. It is inconceivable to me that the framers intended to end capital punishment by the Amendment. *McGautha v. California*, (1971) (separate opinion).

By limiting its grants of certiorari, the Court has refused even to hear argument on the Eighth Amendment claim on two occasions in the last four years. In these cases, the Court confined its attention to the procedural aspects of capital trials, it being implicit that the punishment itself could be constitutionally imposed. Nonetheless, the Court has now been asked to hold that a punishment clearly permissible under the Constitution at the time of its adoption and accepted as such by every member of the Court until today, is suddenly so cruel as to be incompatible with the Eighth Amendment.

Legislatures Should Recognize Social Changes

Before recognizing such an instant evolution in the law, it seems fair to ask what factors have changed that capital punishment should now be "cruel" in the constitutional sense as it has not been in the past. It is apparent that there has been no change of constitutional significance in the nature of the punishment itself. Twentieth century modes of execution surely involve no greater physical suffering than the means employed at the time of the Eighth Amendment's adoption. And although a man awaiting execution must inevitably experience extraordinary mental anguish, no one suggests that this anguish is materially different from that experienced by condemned men in 1791, even though protracted appellate review processes have greatly increased the waiting time on "death row." To be sure, the ordeal of the condemned man may be thought cruel in the sense that all suffering is thought cruel. But if the Constitution proscribed every punishment producing severe emotional stress, then capital punishment would clearly have been impermissible in 1791.

However, the inquiry cannot end here. For reasons unrelated to any change in intrinsic cruelty, the Eighth Amendment prohibition cannot fairly be limited to those punishments thought excessively cruel and barbarous at the time of the adoption of the Eighth Amendment. A punishment is inordinately cruel, in the sense we must deal with it in these cases, chiefly as perceived by the society so characterizing it. The standard of extreme cruelty is not merely descriptive, but necessarily embodies a moral judgment. The standard itself remains the same, but its applicability must change as the basic mores of society change. This notion is not new to Eighth Amendment adjudication. In *Weems v. United States* (1910), the Court referred with apparent approval to the opinion of the commentators that

> [t]he clause of the Constitution ... may be therefore progressive, and is not fastened to the obsolete, but may acquire meaning as public opinion becomes enlightened by a humane justice.

Mr. Chief Justice Warren, writing the plurality opinion in *Trop v. Dulles*, stated, "The Amendment must draw its meaning from the evolving standards of decency that mark the progress of a maturing society." Nevertheless, the Court, up to now, has never actually held that a punishment has become impermissibly cruel due to a shift in the weight of accepted social values; nor has the Court suggested judicially manageable criteria for measuring such a shift in moral consensus.

The Court's quiescence in this area can be attributed to the fact that, in a democratic society, legislatures, not courts, are constituted to respond to the will and consequently the moral values of the people....

The Death Penalty Is Supported by Americans

There are no obvious indications that capital punishment offends the conscience of society to such a degree that our traditional deference to the legislative judgment must be abandoned. It is not a punishment, such as burning at the stake, that everyone would ineffably find to be repugnant to all civilized standards. Nor is it a punishment so roundly condemned that only a few aberrant legislatures have retained it on the statute books. Capital punishment is authorized by statute in 40 States, the District of Columbia, and in the federal courts for the commission of certain crimes. On four occasions in the last 11 years, Congress has added to the list of federal crimes punishable by death. In looking for reliable indicia of contemporary attitude, none more trustworthy has been advanced.

One conceivable source of evidence that legislatures have abdicated their essentially barometric role with respect to community values would be public opinion polls, of which there have been many in the past decade addressed to the question of capital punishment. Without assessing the reliability of such polls, or intimating that any judicial reliance could ever be placed on them, it need only be noted that the reported results have shown nothing approximating the universal condemnation of capital punishment that might lead us to suspect that the legislatures in general have lost touch with current social values.

Counsel for petitioners rely on a different body of empirical evidence. They argue, in effect, that the number of cases in which the death penalty is imposed, as compared with the number of cases in which it is statutorily available, reflects a general revulsion toward the penalty that would lead to its repeal if only it were more generally and widely enforced. It cannot be gainsaid that, by the choice of juries—and sometimes judges—the death penalty is imposed in far fewer than half the cases in which it is available. To go further and characterize the rate of imposition as "freakishly rare," as petitioners insist, is unwarranted hyperbole. And regardless of its characterization, the rate of imposition does not impel the conclusion that capital punishment is now regarded as intolerably cruel or uncivilized. . . .

The rate of imposition of death sentences falls far short of providing the requisite unambiguous evidence that the legislatures of 40 States and the Congress have turned their backs on current or evolving standards of decency in continuing to make the death penalty available. For, if selective imposition evidences a rejection of capital punishment in those cases where it is not imposed, it surely evidences a correlative affirmation of the penalty in those cases where it is imposed. Absent some clear indication that the continued imposition of the death penalty on a selective basis is violative of prevailing standards of civilized conduct, the Eighth Amendment cannot be said to interdict its use. . . .

Capital Punishment Might Be Necessary

Capital punishment has also been attacked as violative of the Eighth Amendment on the ground that it is not needed to achieve legitimate penal aims, and is thus "unnecessarily cruel." As a pure policy matter, this approach has much to recommend it, but it seeks to give a dimension to the Eighth Amendment that it was never intended to have and promotes a line of inquiry that this Court has never before pursued. . . .

By pursuing the necessity approach, it becomes even more apparent that it involves matters outside the purview of the Eighth Amendment. Two of the several aims of punishment are generally associated with capital punishment—retribution and deterrence. It is argued that retribution can be discounted because that, after all, is what the Eighth Amendment seeks to eliminate. There is no authority suggesting that the Eighth Amendment was intended to purge the law of its retributive elements, and the Court has consistently assumed that retribution is a legitimate dimension of the punishment of crimes. Furthermore, responsible legal thinkers of widely varying persuasions have debated the sociological and philosophical aspects of the retribution question for generations, neither side being able to convince the other. It would be reading a great deal into the Eighth Amendment to hold that the punishments authorized by legislatures cannot constitutionally reflect a retributive purpose.

The less esoteric but no less controversial question is whether the death penalty acts as a superior deterrent. Those favoring abolition find no evidence that it does. Those favoring retention start from the intuitive notion that capital punishment should act as the most effective deterrent, and note that there is no convincing evidence that it does not. Escape from this empirical stalemate is sought by placing the burden of proof on the States and concluding that they have failed to demonstrate that capital punishment is a more effective deterrent than life imprisonment. Numerous justifications have been advanced for shifting the burden, and they are not without their rhetorical appeal. However, these arguments are not descended from established constitutional principles, but are born of the urge to bypass an unresolved factual question. Comparative deterrence is not a matter that lends itself to precise measurement; to shift the burden to the States is to provide an illusory solution to an enormously complex problem. If it were proper to put the States to the test of demonstrating the deterrent value of capital punishment, we could just as well ask them to prove the need for life imprisonment or any other punishment. Yet I know of no convincing evidence that life imprisonment is a more effective deterrent than 20 years' imprisonment, or even that a $10 parking ticket is a more effective deterrent than a $5 parking ticket. In fact, there are some who go so far as to challenge the notion that any punishments deter crime. If the States are unable to adduce convincing proof rebutting such assertions, does it then follow that all punishments are suspect as being "cruel and unusual" within the meaning of the Constitution? On the contrary, I submit that the questions raised by the necessity approach are beyond the pale of judicial inquiry under the Eighth Amendment.

Legislatures Must Rethink the Death Penalty

Today the Court has not ruled that capital punishment is *per se* violative of the Eighth Amendment, nor has it ruled that the punishment is barred for any particular class or classes of crimes. The substantially similar concurring opinions of Mr.

Justice Stewart and Mr. Justice White, which are necessary to support the judgment setting aside petitioners' sentences, stop short of reaching the ultimate question. The actual scope of the Court's ruling, which I take to be embodied in these concurring opinions, is not entirely clear. This much, however, seems apparent: if the legislatures are to continue to authorize capital punishment for some crimes, juries and judges can no longer be permitted to make the sentencing determination in the same manner they have in the past. This approach—not urged in oral arguments or briefs—misconceives the nature of the constitutional command against "cruel and unusual punishments," disregards controlling case law, and demands a rigidity in capital cases which, if possible of achievement, cannot be regarded as a welcome change. Indeed the contrary seems to be the case. . . .

While I would not undertake to make a definitive statement as to the parameters of the Court's ruling, it is clear that, if state legislatures and the Congress wish to maintain the availability of capital punishment, significant statutory changes will have to be made. Since the two pivotal concurring opinions turn on the assumption that the punishment of death is now meted out in a random and unpredictable manner, legislative bodies may seek to bring their laws into compliance with the Court's ruling by providing standards for juries and judges to follow in determining the sentence in capital cases or by more narrowly defining the crimes for which the penalty is to be imposed. If such standards can be devised or the crimes more meticulously defined, the result cannot be detrimental. . . .

Since there is no majority of the Court on the ultimate issue presented in these cases, the future of capital punishment in this country has been left in an uncertain limbo. Rather than providing a final and unambiguous answer on the basic constitutional question, the collective impact of the majority's ruling is to demand an undetermined measure of change from the various state legislatures and the Congress. While I cannot endorse the process of decisionmaking that has yielded today's result and the restraints that that result imposes on legislative action, I am not altogether displeased that legislative bodies have been given the opportunity, and indeed unavoidable responsibility, to make a thorough reevaluation of the entire subject of capital punishment. If today's opinions demonstrate nothing else, they starkly show that this is an area where legislatures can act far more effectively than courts.

> "To satisfy the eighth amendment, ... states must develop limits on discretion which assure that death sentences will not be imposed arbitrarily."

Creating New Death Penalty Laws After *Furman*

Harvard Law Review

The Furman *ruling placed the death penalty in legal limbo, and contemporary observers thought it might even have signaled the end of capital punishment in the United States forever. In its wake, those in favor of the death penalty struggled to find ways to make administration of the death penalty acceptable to the Supreme Court. In designing new death penalty statutes to be less arbitrary, however, state legislatures were operating blindly to some extent because the Court had not given exact guidance on how states could apply the death penalty fairly. In an unsigned 1974 article, excerpted here, legal scholars writing in the enormously influential* Harvard Law Review *analyzed the Court's* Furman *decisions in an attempt to provide additional guidance to those lawmakers working to make capital punishment constitutional. The most promising solution was the reduction of the sentencing discretion of judges and juries, the writers of the article suggested. In order to eliminate arbitrariness and discrimination and thereby conform to the Eighth Amendment, the authors concluded that death penalty statutes needed to in*

Harvard Law Review, "Discretion and the Constitutionality of the New Death Penalty Statutes," vol. 87, June 1974, p. 1,690. Copyright © 1974 by The Harvard Law Review Association. Reproduced by permission of the Harvard Law Review Association and the William S. Hein Company.

clude strict rules guiding when judges or juries could impose the penalty.

In *Furman v. Georgia* the Supreme Court held that the "imposition and carrying out of the death penalty in [the cases at bar] constitutes cruel and unusual punishment in violation of the Eighth and Fourteenth Amendments." The Court's decision, announced in a brief per curiam order accompanied by five concurring and four dissenting opinions, had an immediate impact: on the same day *Furman* was decided the Court vacated death sentences imposed in twenty-six states under a wide range of statutory schemes. Moreover, as two of the dissenters pointed out, the decision mandated the invalidation of statutes enacted by thirty-nine states and by the federal government, and the reversal of death sentences which had been imposed in over 600 cases.

Because each member of the *Furman* majority wrote a separate opinion, the precise scope of the decision is unclear. The Court did not hold, however, that capital punishment per se violated the eighth amendment, since three members of the majority limited their opinions to statutes which allowed sentencing authorities uncontrolled discretion in capital cases. Thus, the decision did not preclude Congress and state legislatures from attempting to enact constitutionally acceptable death penalty laws, and in the two years since *Furman*, more than half the states have enacted statutes which either specify the factors to be weighed by the sentencers in deciding when to impose a capital sentence or require the death penalty for certain offenses. Five state supreme courts have upheld the constitutionality of death sentences imposed under such procedures and over ninety-five people in sixteen states now await execution. . . .

The Court Objects to Arbitrariness

The opinions of Justices [William] Brennan and [Thurgood] Marshall, which concluded that capital punishment per se violates the constitution, provide no guidance in determining what types of death penalty statute would satisfy *Furman*. Moreover, generalizations about the three other concurring opinions must be tentative, since no two Justices joined in any one opinion. Nonetheless, Justices [William] Douglas, [Potter] Stewart, and [Byron] White seem to share a belief that the eighth amendment forbids the arbitrary imposition of capital punishment; their opinions do not make clear, however, whether the statutes were found constitutionally infirm because of actual, proven arbitrariness in the administration of the death penalty by sentencers, or because of the potential for arbitrariness inherent in granting sentencers uncontrolled discretion in deciding when to impose capital punishment.

Much of the language in the *Furman* opinions supports an interpretation which focuses on the manner in which the statutes were administered. . . .

If the constitutional defect in the statutes condemned by *Furman* were arbitrariness, then statutes which are nonarbitrary in operation would be constitutionally acceptable. Such a nonarbitrariness test of the constitutionality of new statutes recently has been adopted by one state supreme court and has been approved by several commentators. But although this interpretation is closely tied to the constitutional evil discussed by Justices Douglas, Stewart, and White, it raises two serious difficulties.

Discrimination Is Hard to Prove

First, while an "arbitrariness-in-fact" test seems to require an empirical foundation, no member of the *Furman* majority was able to demonstrate convincingly that capital punishment had been imposed arbitrarily. Despite their empirical assertions, Justices Stewart and White presented little statistical data to support their observations, and Justice Douglas' evidence did not isolate the sentencing authority as the source of the racial and class discrimination he perceived. Moreover, the same day *Furman* was decided the Court summarily vacated, without individual findings of arbitrariness, death sentences imposed in twenty-six states, including sentences imposed under a statute which had been in effect for less than two years.

Second, an arbitrariness test would require courts to predict, without empirical foundation, the extent of arbitrariness likely to result under a statutory scheme. For courts untroubled by the lack of data, determining constitutionality would depend on quite speculative prophecies based on little more than evaluating the amount of discretion delegated to sentencers. For courts unwilling to indulge in such speculation, the lack of data would likely make the outcome depend almost solely on the allocation of the burden of producing evidence.

The Court Should Limit Discretion

These difficulties can be avoided by interpreting *Furman* to condemn statutes which on their face permit sentencers to exercise unfettered discretion. . . .

Although the three concurring opinions do not focus primarily on discretion in sentencing as the constitutional infirmity, Justice Douglas acknowledged that discrimination against individual petitioners could not be proved, and he contended that judicial intervention was warranted because the statutes gave "uncontrolled discretion" to sentencers and provided "no standards [to] govern the selection of the penalty." The eighth amendment, he concluded, "require[s] legislatures to write penal laws" that are not arbitrary on their face. Similarly, parts of Justice Stewart's opinion can be read to be concerned with discretion in the sentencing process. Moreover, several courts, in rejecting attempts to prove that pre-*Furman* laws were administered nonarbitrarily and in scrutinizing new death penalty statutes, have looked to the amount of discretion in the statutes to determine whether they were constitutional. Thus, a "discretion-per-se" reading of *Furman* is not without support in the concurring opinions and in subsequent decisions, and, as compared with an "arbitrariness-in-fact" interpretation, avoids a number of difficulties.

If *Furman v. Georgia* is properly understood as an attack on sentencing discretion in capital cases, then before scrutinizing new death statutes, courts must first determine how much discretion need be eliminated to satisfy the eighth amendment. Some courts have concluded that *Furman* requires elimination of all sentencing discretion. However, implementing so absolute an interpretation may be neither feasible nor desirable. Structuring discretion cannot completely eliminate inconsistent treatment in sentencing of criminal offenders, and attempts to achieve maximum confinement of discretion may eliminate valuable discretion which permits individualization without appreciably reducing the likelihood of arbitrary results and state complicity therein. Such costs would be excessive, particularly if, as Justice White suggested, the proper approach in construing the reach of the eighth amendment rests upon a balance of competing interests.

Courts Need Clear Guidelines

Recent decisions limiting agency discretion in order to prevent administrative arbitrariness suggest that less drastic means to structure and control sentencing discretion may be constitutionally acceptable. Rather than attempting to eliminate all administrative freedom, courts increasingly have required state and federal administrative agencies to promulgate specific guidelines to limit their own discretion. For example, courts have compelled administrators to prescribe rules or standards to be followed in deciding who should be paroled, who shall be subjected to disciplinary action for "unprofessional conduct," or what criminal evidence shall be preserved for use by defendants. Guidelines once promulgated bind the agency, and actions which are contrary to the guidelines are subject to reversal. These decisions all rest on the assumption that arbitrariness can be substantially eradicated by requiring standards or rules to guide the decision-maker and judicial review to assure that the standards are followed. Professor [Kenneth C.] Davis, the leading advocate of limiting administrative discretion, has labeled the process "confining, structuring, and checking" and has suggested that this process should be applied in criminal proceedings. . . .

Not every attempt to curb sentencing discretion will satisfy the eighth amendment, however. Structuring discretion by establishing sentencing standards requires more than specifying vague sentencing criteria, as the Supreme Court implicitly recognized in vacating sentences imposed under laws which provided a non-exhaustive list of general criteria to guide the sentencer. . . . To satisfy the eighth amendment, therefore, states must develop limits on discretion which assure that death sentences will not be imposed arbitrarily.

CHAPTER 2

Reinstituting and Regulating the Death Penalty

Chapter Preface

Case Overview: *Gregg v. Georgia* (1976)

After the Supreme Court's ruling in *Furman v. Georgia* in 1972 that capital punishment, as then applied in the United States, violated the Eighth Amendment's protection against cruel and unusual punishment, legislators in state and federal governments began working to create criminal statutes that would allow for the existence of a fair and nonarbitrary death penalty. It remained unclear whether a majority of the justices would ever be willing to find capital punishment constitutional, but legislators crafting new statutes took their cues from Chief Justice Warren Burger's dissenting opinion and Justice Potter Stewart's concurring opinion, both of which had implied that a less arbitrary death penalty might find favor with the Court. Once these new statutes were written and applied, they were challenged on appeal through the court system until they reached the Supreme Court.

The first case to reach the Court was that of Troy Gregg, who had been sentenced to death in Georgia after he was found guilty of the 1973 murders of Fred Simmons and Bob Moore, two men who had given Gregg and his friend Floyd Allen a ride from Florida to Georgia. Gregg and Allen were identified by another hitchhiker, and when the police ultimately captured the suspects they found the murder weapon in Gregg's pocket. While Gregg argued that he had shot Simmons and Moore in self-defense, Allen stated that Gregg had carefully planned and carried out the killings in order to steal the car.

Under the new Georgia statutes, capital trials were divided into two parts: a criminal phase, during which the jury determined the guilt or innocence of defendants, and a penalty phase, during which the jury decided on appropriate punishments for those defendants found guilty. In the penalty phase of trials, during which the convicted defendants could testify without fear of incriminating themselves, juries were free to consider all aggravating or mitigating circumstances; under the Georgia laws, moreover, defendants could not be sentenced to death unless the jury found beyond a reasonable doubt that at least one of ten statutory aggravating circumstances had been met.

Neither the prosecution nor the defense presented additional evidence during Gregg's penalty phase; both instead argued about the rectitude of the death penalty itself. The jury found two aggravating circumstances (that Gregg had committed the murders while he was engaged in the commission of two other capital felonies and had killed in order to take the victims' property). Accordingly Gregg was sentenced to death. Under Georgia's new laws, once the jury had decided to impose the death penalty Gregg's case was automatically appealed to the supreme court of Georgia, which was instructed by statute to determine whether the sentence had been imposed fairly. The supreme court of Georgia affirmed both the convictions and the imposition of the death sentences for murder. The U.S. Supreme Court then agreed to consider the case, largely to address the questions *Furman* had left unanswered about whether capital punishment could ever be constitutional.

Ruling in *Gregg v. Georgia*, the Court declared 7-2 that Georgia's death penalty statutes provided sufficient "guided discretion" for jurors deliberating whether to sentence offenders to death to eliminate arbitrariness. Therefore, they concluded, the death penalty violated neither the Eighth Amendment prohibition against cruel and unusual punishment nor the Fourteenth Amendment guarantee of equal protection, and Gregg's death sentence should stand. Delivering the plurality opinion, Justices Potter Stewart, Lewis F. Powell, and John Paul Stevens (two of whom had voted to strike down capital punishment in *Furman*) argued that the fact that thirty-five states had passed legislation after *Furman* to reinstate the death penalty indicated that the majority of American society approved of capital punishment. Concerns about the arbitrary nature of the death penalty, they concluded, could be answered by carefully written laws that provided adequate guidance and information to juries and that preferably allowed for two-part trials. Justice Byron White, Chief Justice Warren Burger, and Justice William H. Rehnquist similarly agreed that Georgia's new laws were rigorous enough to ensure that the death penalty was being applied in a fair, impassionate manner, and that the death penalty itself did not automatically constitute cruel and unusual punishment. Justice Harry Blackmun added a short opinion pointing out that *Gregg* complemented *Furman* by speaking to the need for a fair and evenhanded system of justice.

Two members of the Court dissented from the decision. Justice Thurgood Marshall restated his opinion in *Furman* that the death penalty was by its very nature cruel and unusual. Justice William Brennan declared that "evolving standards of decency" in the United States had reached a point where capital punishment, while it was once acceptable, should be declared unconstitutional.

> "We now hold that the punishment of death does not invariably violate the Constitution."

The Court's Opinion: A Properly Directed Death Penalty Is Constitutional

Potter Stewart

In the Supreme Court's plurality opinion in Gregg v. Georgia, *excerpted here, Justices Potter Stewart, Lewis F. Powell Jr., and John Paul Stevens upheld Troy Gregg's death sentence. This ruling had the effect of reversing the Court's finding in* Furman v. Georgia *(1972) that the death penalty, as then applied in the United States, constituted a cruel and unusual punishment. In* Gregg *the Court found that the death penalty laws established by Georgia in the wake of* Furman *were constitutional, thereby validating similar laws throughout the country. The justices first dealt with the overarching question of the permissibility of capital punishment by noting that the death penalty is not necessarily unconstitutional, as it does not automatically violate the Eighth and Fourteenth Amendments. Citing post-*Furman *election and opinion poll results, the justices then argued that public opinion in the United States was in favor of capital punishment. Therefore, they concluded, the death penalty was consistent with society's evolving standards for the humane treatment of convicts. Moreover, they added, the new Georgia statutes were sufficiently rigorous so as to ensure that the death penalty would not be arbitrarily applied; as such, the death penalty could no longer be considered "cruel and unusual." Stewart was nominated to*

Potter Stewart, plurality opinion, *Gregg v. Georgia*, U.S. Supreme Court, July 2, 1976.

59

the Supreme Court by President Dwight D. Eisenhower in October 1958 and served as an associate justice until his retirement in 1981.

The issue in this case is whether the imposition of the sentence of death for the crime of murder under the law of Georgia violates the Eighth and Fourteenth Amendments....

We address initially the basic contention that the punishment of death for the crime of murder is, under all circumstances, "cruel and unusual" in violation of the Eighth and Fourteenth Amendments of the Constitution....

We now hold that the punishment of death does not invariably violate the Constitution....

The Death Penalty Has Long Been Accepted

We now consider specifically whether the sentence of death for the crime of murder is a per se violation of the Eighth and Fourteenth Amendments to the Constitution. We note first that history and precedent strongly support a negative answer to this question.

The imposition of the death penalty for the crime of murder has a long history of acceptance both in the United States and in England. The common law rule imposed a mandatory death sentence on all convicted murderers. And the penalty continued to be used into the 20th century by most American States, although the breadth of the common law rule was diminished, initially by narrowing the class of murders to be punished by death and subsequently by widespread adoption of laws expressly granting juries the discretion to recommend mercy.

It is apparent from the text of the Constitution itself that the existence of capital punishment was accepted by the Framers. At the time the Eighth Amendment was ratified, capital punishment was a common sanction in every State. Indeed, the First Congress of the United States enacted legislation providing death as the penalty for specified crimes. The Fifth Amendment, adopted at the same time as the Eighth, contemplated the continued existence of the capital sanction by imposing certain limits on the prosecution of capital cases: "No person shall be held to answer for a capital, or otherwise infamous crime, unless on a presentment or indictment of a Grand Jury . . .; nor shall any person be subject for the same offense to be twice put in jeopardy of life or limb; . . . nor be deprived of life, liberty, or property, without due process of law. . . ."

And the Fourteenth Amendment, adopted over three-quarters of a century later, similarly contemplates the existence of the capital sanction in providing that no State shall deprive any person of "life, liberty, or property" without due process of law.

For nearly two centuries, this Court, repeatedly and often expressly, has recognized that capital punishment is not invalid per se. . . .

Community Standards Have Not Changed

Four years ago, the petitioners in *Furman* and its companion cases predicated their argument primarily upon the asserted proposition that standards of decency had evolved to the point where capital punishment no longer could be tolerated. The petitioners in those cases said, in effect, that the evolutionary process had come to an end, and that standards of decency required that the Eighth Amendment be construed finally as prohibiting capital punishment for any crime, regardless of its depravity and impact on society. This view was accepted by two Justices. Three other Justices were unwilling to go so far; focusing on the procedures by which convicted defendants were selected for the death penalty, rather than on the actual punishment inflicted, they joined in the conclusion that the statutes before the Court were constitutionally invalid.

The petitioners in the capital cases before the Court today renew the "standards of decency" argument, but developments during the four years since *Furman* have undercut substantially the assumptions upon which their argument rested. Despite the continuing debate, dating back to the 19th century, over the morality and utility of capital punishment, it is now evident that a large proportion of American society continues to regard it as an appropriate and necessary criminal sanction.

The most marked indication of society's endorsement of the death penalty for murder is the legislative response to *Furman*. The legislatures of at least 35 States have enacted new statutes that provide for the death penalty for at least some crimes that result in the death of another person. And the Congress of the United States, in 1974, enacted a statute providing the death penalty for aircraft piracy that results in death.

As we have seen, however, the Eighth Amendment demands more than that a challenged punishment be acceptable to contemporary society. The Court also must ask whether it comports with the basic concept of human dignity at the core of the Amendment. Although we cannot "invalidate a category of penalties because we deem less severe penalties adequate to serve the ends of penology," *Furman v. Georgia*, ([Lewis] Powell, dissenting), the sanction imposed cannot be so totally without penological justification that it results in the gratuitous infliction of suffering.

Retribution

The death penalty is said to serve two principal social purposes: retribution and deterrence of capital crimes by prospective offenders.

In part, capital punishment is an expression of society's moral outrage at particularly offensive conduct. This function may be unappealing to many, but it is essential in an ordered

Reinstituting and Regulating the Death Penalty

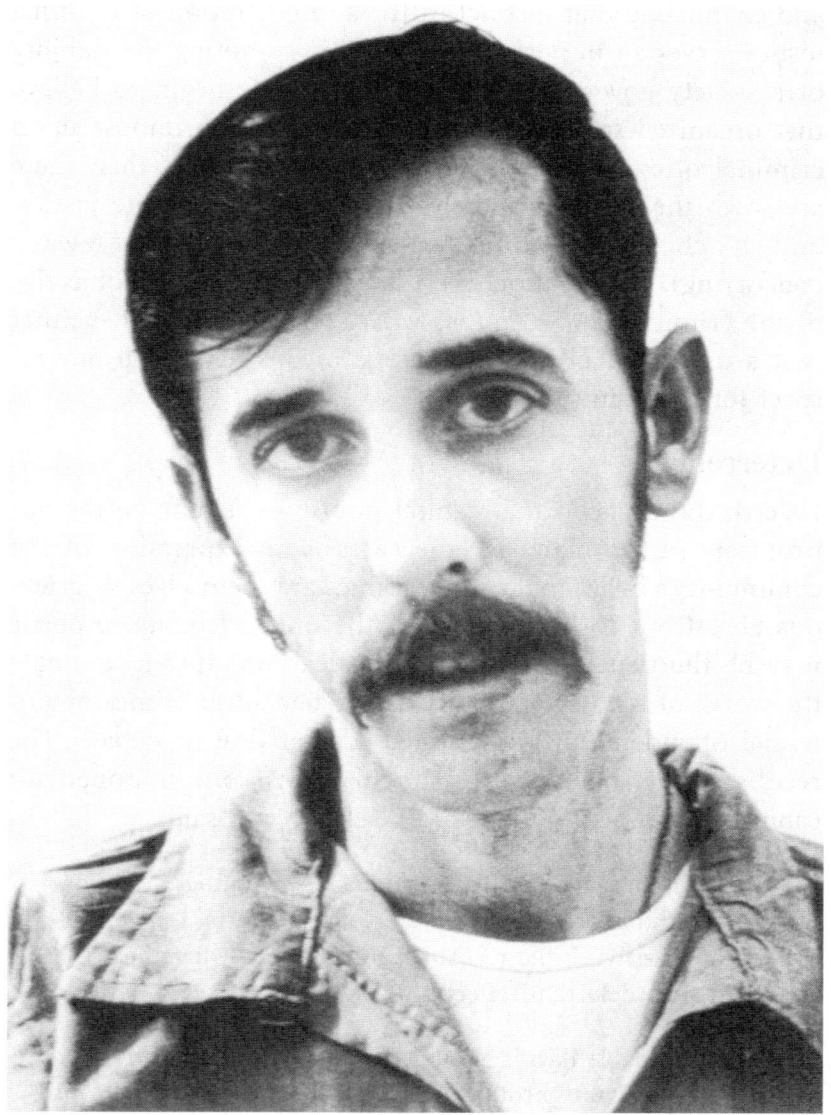

The Supreme court upheld Troy Gregg's death sentence for murdering two men who gave him and a companion a ride. © The Bettmann Archives/CORBIS

society that asks its citizens to rely on legal processes, rather than self-help, to vindicate their wrongs.

"The instinct for retribution is part of the nature of man,

and channeling that instinct in the administration of criminal justice serves an important purpose in promoting the stability of a society governed by law. When people begin to believe that organized society is unwilling or unable to impose upon criminal offenders the punishment they 'deserve,' then there are sown the seeds of anarchy—of self-help, vigilante justice, and lynch law." *Furman v. Georgia* ([Potter] Stewart, concurring). "Retribution is no longer the dominant objective of the criminal law," *Williams v. New York* (1949), but neither is it a forbidden objective, nor one inconsistent with our respect for the dignity of men.

Deterrence

Indeed, the decision that capital punishment may be the appropriate sanction in extreme cases is an expression of the community's belief that certain crimes are themselves so grievous an affront to humanity that the only adequate response may be the penalty of death. Statistical attempts to evaluate the worth of the death penalty as a deterrent to crimes by potential offenders have occasioned a great deal of debate. The results simply have been inconclusive. As one opponent of capital punishment [Charles L. Black, Jr.] has said:

> [A]fter all possible inquiry, including the probing of all possible methods of inquiry, we do not know, and, for systematic and easily visible reasons, cannot know, what the truth about this "deterrent" effect may be....
>
> The inescapable flaw is ... that social conditions in any state are not constant through time, and that social conditions are not the same in any two states. If an effect were observed (and the observed effects, one way or another, are not large), then one could not at all tell whether any of this effect is attributable to the presence or absence of capital punishment. A "scientific"—that is to say, a soundly based—conclusion is simply impossible, and no methodological path out of this tangle suggests itself.

Although some of the studies suggest that the death penalty may not function as a significantly greater deterrent than lesser penalties, there is no convincing empirical evidence either supporting or refuting this view. We may nevertheless assume safely that there are murderers, such as those who act in passion, for whom the threat of death has little or no deterrent effect. But for many others, the death penalty undoubtedly is a significant deterrent. There are carefully contemplated murders, such as murder for hire, where the possible penalty of death may well enter into the cold calculus that precedes the decision to act. And there are some categories of murder, such as murder by a life prisoner, where other sanctions may not be adequate.

The value of capital punishment as a deterrent of crime is a complex factual issue the resolution of which properly rests with the legislatures, which can evaluate the results of statistical studies in terms of their own local conditions and with a flexibility of approach that is not available to the courts. Indeed, many of the post-*Furman* statutes reflect just such a responsible effort to define those crimes and those criminals for which capital punishment is most probably an effective deterrent.

Not Unconstitutionally Severe

In sum, we cannot say that the judgment of the Georgia Legislature that capital punishment may be necessary in some cases is clearly wrong. Considerations of federalism, as well as respect for the ability of a legislature to evaluate, in terms of its particular State, the moral consensus concerning the death penalty and its social utility as a sanction, require us to conclude, in the absence of more convincing evidence, that the infliction of death as a punishment for murder is not without justification, and thus is not unconstitutionally severe.

Finally, we must consider whether the punishment of death is disproportionate in relation to the crime for which it is imposed. There is no question that death, as a punishment, is unique in its severity and irrevocability. When a defendant's life is at stake, the Court has been particularly sensitive to insure that every safeguard is observed. But we are concerned here only with the imposition of capital punishment for the crime of murder, and, when a life has been taken deliberately by the offender, we cannot say that the punishment is invariably disproportionate to the crime. It is an extreme sanction, suitable to the most extreme of crimes.

We hold that the death penalty is not a form of punishment that may never be imposed, regardless of the circumstances of the offense, regardless of the character of the offender, and regardless of the procedure followed in reaching the decision to impose it.

We now consider whether Georgia may impose the death penalty on the petitioner in this case.

Jury Guidance Can Ensure Fairness

While *Furman* did not hold that the infliction of the death penalty per se violates the Constitution's ban on cruel and unusual punishments, it did recognize that the penalty of death is different in kind from any other punishment imposed under our system of criminal justice. Because of the uniqueness of the death penalty, *Furman* held that it could not be imposed under sentencing procedures that created a substantial risk that it would be inflicted in an arbitrary and capricious manner. . . .

Furman mandates that, where discretion is afforded a sentencing body on a matter so grave as the determination of whether a human life should be taken or spared, that discretion must be suitably directed and limited so as to minimize the risk of wholly arbitrary and capricious action. . . .

Jury sentencing has been considered desirable in capital cases in order "to maintain a link between contemporary community values and the penal system—a link without which the determination of punishment could hardly reflect 'the evolving standards of decency that mark the progress of a maturing society'" [as stated in *Witherspoon v. Illinois*].

But it creates special problems. Much of the information that is relevant to the sentencing decision may have no relevance to the question of guilt, or may even be extremely prejudicial to a fair determination of that question. This problem, however, is scarcely insurmountable. Those who have studied the question suggest that a bifurcated procedure—one in which the question of sentence is not considered until the determination of guilt has been made—is the best answer....

The idea that a jury should be given guidance in its decisionmaking is also hardly a novel proposition. Juries are invariably given careful instructions on the law and how to apply it before they are authorized to decide the merits of a lawsuit. It would be virtually unthinkable to follow any other course in a legal system that has traditionally operated by following prior precedents and fixed rules of law. When erroneous instructions are given, retrial is often required. It is quite simply a hallmark of our legal system that juries be carefully and adequately guided in their deliberations.

While some have suggested that standards to guide a capital jury's sentencing deliberations are impossible to formulate, the fact is that such standards have been developed....

While such standards are, by necessity, somewhat general, they do provide guidance to the sentencing authority, and thereby reduce the likelihood that it will impose a sentence that fairly can be called capricious or arbitrary. Where the sentencing authority is required to specify the factors it relied upon in reaching its decision, the further safeguard of meaningful appellate review is available to ensure that death sentences are not imposed capriciously or in a freakish manner.

In summary, the concerns expressed in *Furman* that the penalty of death not be imposed in an arbitrary or capricious manner can be met by a carefully drafted statute that ensures that the sentencing authority is given adequate information and guidance. As a general proposition, these concerns are best met by a system that provides for a bifurcated proceeding at which the sentencing authority is apprised of the information relevant to the imposition of sentence and provided with standards to guide its use of the information. . . .

No longer can a Georgia jury do as Furman's jury did: reach a finding of the defendant's guilt and then, without guidance or direction, decide whether he should live or die. Instead, the jury's attention is directed to the specific circumstances of the crime: was it committed in the course of another capital felony? Was it committed for money? Was it committed upon a peace officer or judicial officer? Was it committed in a particularly heinous way, or in a manner that endangered the lives of many persons? In addition, the jury's attention is focused on the characteristics of the person who committed the crime: does he have a record of prior convictions for capital offenses? Are there any special facts about this defendant that mitigate against imposing capital punishment (e.g., his youth, the extent of his cooperation with the police, his emotional state at the time of the crime)? As a result, while some jury discretion still exists, "the discretion to be exercised is controlled by clear and objective standards so as to produce nondiscriminatory application." *Coley v. State* (1974). . . .

Georgia's New Laws Are Constitutional

The basic concern of *Furman* centered on those defendants who were being condemned to death capriciously and arbitrarily. Under the procedures before the Court in that case, sentencing authorities were not directed to give attention to the nature or circumstances of the crime committed or to the character or record of the defendant. Left unguided, juries imposed the death sentence in a way that could only be called freakish. The new Georgia sentencing procedures, by contrast, focus the jury's attention on the particularized nature of the crime and the particularized characteristics of the individual defendant. While the jury is permitted to consider any aggravating or mitigating circumstances, it must find and identify at least one statutory aggravating factor before it may impose a penalty of death. In this way, the jury's discretion is channeled. No longer can a jury wantonly and freakishly impose the death sentence; it is always circumscribed by the legislative guidelines. In addition, the review function of the Supreme Court of Georgia affords additional assurance that the concerns that prompted our decision in *Furman* are not present to any significant degree in the Georgia procedure applied here.

For the reasons expressed in this opinion, we hold that the statutory system under which Gregg was sentenced to death does not violate the Constitution. Accordingly, the judgment of the Georgia Supreme Court is affirmed.

It is so ordered.

> "The opinions of an informed public would differ significantly from those of a public unaware of the consequences and effects of the death penalty."

Dissenting Opinion: The Death Penalty Remains an Excessive Penalty

Thurgood Marshall

In his dissenting opinion in Gregg v. Georgia, *excerpted here, Justice Thurgood Marshall, the first African American on the Supreme Court and one of the Court's most liberal members, argued that the death penalty represents "cruel and unusual" punishment and therefore is in all cases unconstitutional. Acknowledging that opinion polls seemed to suggest that the American public supported capital punishment, Marshall continued to maintain, as he had in* Furman v. Georgia *(1972), that if Americans were aware of the true nature of the death penalty they would reject capital punishment forever. Ultimately, Marshall concluded, the death penalty is an excessive punishment, as it neither helps deter criminals nor serves "any legitimate notion" of retribution. Marshall was appointed to the Supreme Court by President Lyndon B. Johnson in 1967; he served as an associate justice until his retirement in 1991.*

In *Furman v. Georgia* (1972) (concurring opinion), I set forth at some length my views on the basic issue presented to the Court in these cases. The death penalty, I concluded, is

Thurgood Marshall, dissenting opinion, *Gregg v. Georgia*, U.S. Supreme Court, July 2, 1976.

a cruel and unusual punishment prohibited by the Eighth and Fourteenth Amendments. That continues to be my view.

I have no intention of retracing the "long and tedious journey" that led to my conclusion in *Furman*. My sole purposes here are to consider the suggestion that my conclusion in *Furman* has been undercut by developments since then, and briefly to evaluate the basis for my Brethren's holding that the extinction of life is a permissible form of punishment under the Cruel and Unusual Punishments Clause.

In *Furman*, I concluded that the death penalty is constitutionally invalid for two reasons. First, the death penalty is excessive. And second, the American people, fully informed as to the purposes of the death penalty and its liabilities, would, in my view, reject it as morally unacceptable.

Since the decision in *Furman*, the legislatures of 35 States have enacted new statutes authorizing the imposition of the death sentence for certain crimes, and Congress has enacted a law providing the death penalty for air piracy resulting in death. I would be less than candid if I did not acknowledge that these developments have a significant bearing on a realistic assessment of the moral acceptability of the death penalty to the American people. But if the constitutionality of the death penalty turns, as I have urged, on the opinion of an informed citizenry, then even the enactment of new death statutes cannot be viewed as conclusive. In *Furman*, I observed that the American people are largely unaware of the information critical to a judgment on the morality of the death penalty, and concluded that, if they were better informed, they would consider it shocking, unjust, and unacceptable. A recent study, conducted after the enactment of the post-*Furman* statutes, has confirmed that the American people know little about the death penalty, and that the opinions of an informed public would differ significantly from those of a public unaware of the consequences and effects of the death penalty.

The Death Penalty Remains Excessive

Even assuming, however, that the post-*Furman* enactment of statutes authorizing the death penalty renders the prediction of the views of an informed citizenry an uncertain basis for a constitutional decision, the enactment of those statutes has no bearing whatsoever on the conclusion that the death penalty is unconstitutional because it is excessive. An excessive penalty is invalid under the Cruel and Unusual Punishments Clause "even though popular sentiment may favor" it [as stated in Marshall's concurring opinion in *Furman*]. The inquiry here, then, is simply whether the death penalty is necessary to accomplish the legitimate legislative purposes in punishment, or whether a less severe penalty—life imprisonment—would do as well.

The two purposes that sustain the death penalty as nonexcessive in the Court's view are general deterrence and retribution. In *Furman*, I canvassed the relevant data on the deterrent effect of capital punishment. The state of knowledge at that point, after literally centuries of debate, was summarized as follows by a United Nations Committee:

> It is generally agreed between the retentionists and abolitionists, whatever their opinions about the validity of comparative studies of deterrence, that the data which now exist show no correlation between the existence of capital punishment and lower rates of capital crime.

The available evidence, I concluded in *Furman*, was convincing that "capital punishment is not necessary as a deterrent to crime in our society."

The Notion of Retribution

The other principal purpose said to be served by the death penalty is retribution. The notion that retribution can serve as a moral justification for the sanction of death finds credence in the opinion of my Brothers Stewart, Powell, and Stevens, and that of my Brother White in *Roberts v. Louisiana*. It is this notion that I find to be the most disturbing aspect of today's unfortunate decisions.

The concept of retribution is a multifaceted one, and any discussion of its role in the criminal law must be undertaken with caution. On one level, it can be said that the notion of retribution or reprobation is the basis of our insistence that only those who have broken the law be punished, and, in this sense, the notion is quite obviously central to a just system of criminal sanctions. But our recognition that retribution plays a crucial role in determining who may be punished by no means requires approval of retribution as a general justification for punishment. It is the question whether retribution can provide a moral justification for punishment—in particular, capital punishment—that we must consider.

My Brothers Stewart, Powell, and Stevens offer the following explanation of the retributive justification for capital punishment:

> The instinct for retribution is part of the nature of man, and channeling that instinct in the administration of criminal justice serves an important purpose in promoting the stability of a society governed by law. When people begin to believe that organized society is unwilling or unable to impose upon criminal offenders the punishment they "deserve," then there are sown the seeds of anarchy—of self-help, vigilante justice, and lynch law. *Furman v. Georgia* (Stewart, J., concurring).

Inadequate Justification

This statement is wholly inadequate to justify the death penalty. As my Brother Brennan stated in *Furman*, "[t]here is no evidence whatever that utilization of imprisonment, rather than death, encourages private blood feuds and other disorders."

It simply defies belief to suggest that the death penalty is necessary to prevent the American people from taking the law into their own hands.

In a related vein, it may be suggested that the expression of moral outrage through the imposition of the death penalty serves to reinforce basic moral values—that it marks some crimes as particularly offensive, and therefore to be avoided. The argument is akin to a deterrence argument, but differs in that it contemplates the individual's shrinking from antisocial conduct not because he fears punishment, but because he has been told in the strongest possible way that the conduct is wrong. This contention, like the previous one, provides no support for the death penalty. It is inconceivable that any individual concerned about conforming his conduct to what society says is "right" would fail to realize that murder is "wrong" if the penalty were simply life imprisonment.

The foregoing contentions—that society's expression of moral outrage through the imposition of the death penalty preempts the citizenry from taking the law into its own hands and reinforces moral values—are not retributive in the purest sense. They are essentially utilitarian, in that they portray the death penalty as valuable because of its beneficial results. These justifications for the death penalty are inadequate because the penalty is, quite clearly I think, not necessary to the accomplishment of those results.

Society's Judgment Is Insufficient

There remains for consideration, however, what might be termed the purely retributive justification for the death penalty—that the death penalty is appropriate not because of its beneficial effect on society, but because the taking of the murderer's life is itself morally good. Some of the language of the opinion of my Brothers Stewart, Powell, and Stevens appears positively to embrace this notion of retribution for its own sake as a justification for capital punishment. They state:

> [T]he decision that capital punishment may be the appropriate sanction in extreme cases is an expression of the community's belief that certain crimes are themselves so grievous an affront to humanity that the only adequate response may be the penalty of death.

They then quote with approval from Lord Justice Denning's remarks before the British Royal Commission on Capital Punishment:

> The truth is that some crimes are so outrageous that society insists on adequate punishment because the wrongdoer deserves it, irrespective of whether it is a deterrent or not.

Of course, it may be that these statements are intended as no more than observations as to the popular demands that it is thought must be responded to in order to prevent anarchy. But the implication of the statements appears to me to be quite different—namely, that society's judgment that the murderer "deserves" death must be respected not simply because the preservation of order requires it, but because it is appropriate that society make the judgment and carry it out. It is this latter notion, in particular, that I consider to be fundamentally at odds with the Eighth Amendment. The mere fact that the community demands the murderer's life in return for the evil he has done cannot sustain the death penalty, for as Justices Stewart, Powell, and Stevens remind us [in *Furman*], "the Eighth Amendment demands more than that a challenged punishment be acceptable to contemporary society." To be sustained under the Eighth Amendment, the death penalty must "compor[t] with the basic concept of human dignity at the core of the Amendment"; the objective in imposing it must be "[consistent] with our respect for the dignity of [other] men." Under these standards, the taking of life "because the wrongdoer deserves it" surely must fall, for such a punishment has as its very basis the total denial of the wrongdoer's dignity and worth.

The Death Penalty

The death penalty, unnecessary to promote the goal of deterrence or to further any legitimate notion of retribution, is an excessive penalty forbidden by the Eighth and Fourteenth Amendments. I respectfully dissent from the Court's judgment upholding the sentences of death imposed upon the petitioners in these cases.

"The return of the death penalty to American justice promises to be morally invigorating, except of course to those chosen few who get killed by it."

The Death Penalty Is Still Arbitrary

William Greider

In a 1976 editorial published shortly after the Supreme Court's decision in Gregg v. Georgia *(and excerpted here), journalist William Greider argued that even under the new death penalty statutes approved by the Court, capital punishment remained arbitrary. More disturbing, Greider added, was the suggestion that the renewed death penalty was being applied in a racist fashion and would result in the execution of a disproportionate number of African American offenders. Greider, an experienced political writer and author of a number of books and articles, is currently the national affairs correspondent for the* Nation, *a liberal journal of opinon.*

The return of the death penalty to American justice promises to be morally invigorating, except of course to those chosen few who get killed by it.

Executions remind us of familiar scenes from old movies, Jimmy Cagney walking the last mile, gamely, a priest chanting at his elbow, his widow-to-be weeping in the warden's office. Cagney always dies so well: no convulsions, no popping of the eyeballs.

William Greider, "The Return of the Death Penalty," *Washington Post*, November 28, 1976. Copyright © 1976 by the *Washington Post*. Reproduced by permission.

And the issue of capital punishment revives the easy passions of high school debating. The old imponderable topics are all before us again. Resolved: that sudden death is far better than life in a prison cell. Resolved: that premeditated killing by society brutalizes its own citizens. Resolved: that the criminal mind is deterred by only one thing, fear of death.

The first few executions should make exciting news; no prisoner has been executed in America since 1967 and now there are going to be lots of them. It's only a matter of weeks or months until somebody "burns," as the prisoners put it, wherever the defense lawyers exhaust the stalling tactics and the last stay expires.

Since there will be so many of them—about 350 people are already under death sentence and many more are in the judicial pipeline—the repetition of electrocutions and hangings may eventually seem routine, even boring.

What promises to keep the subject permanently stimulating is a less obvious question, a legal contention which a small but zealous network of abolitionist lawyers intends to pursue for months or years, whatever it takes. The question is: Which murderers shall society select for death, which murderers shall be allowed to live?

The U.S. Supreme Court presumably settled that matter last summer when it upheld the new death-penalty laws enacted by Georgia, Florida and Texas as fair—statutes which define capital crimes more precisely and guide the discretion of prosecutors, juries and judges in applying the ultimate punishment. Most other states, guided by that decision, are proceeding with similar laws.

The Georgia Experience

But the abolitionists—the NAACP Legal Defense Fund, the American Civil Liberties Union and like-minded groups—will be heard from again. In time, they predict, they will be back at the Supreme Court, arguing that the new laws are as unfair as the old ones, that the selection for execution is a random game, arbitrary and discriminatory.

In their view, the Supreme Court has authorized a grisly legal experiment in which a number of people will be killed before the issue of fairness can be settled, before the public appetite for executions turns to disgust.

Millard Farmer, Atlanta defense lawyer, specialist in beating the death penalty, team leader for the Southern Poverty Law Center, is confident of this:

"I really think the Supreme Court will realize that they did take the wrong step. The death penalty will be so narrowly defined that it will go down the tubes. But it's going to be a lot of bloody years before that comes to pass."

Georgia is one laboratory for the experiment, an appropriate place to test the question of fairness because Georgia has killed more people in its electric chair than any other state—414 of them since 1924. Only 77 of those people were white. Of 61 men executed for rape, only three were white.

At the moment, Georgia has 66 people under death sentence, according to the unofficial scorecard kept by the ACLU. Among those, 6 out of every 10 are black. Five out of every 6 are poor, unable to hire their own lawyers. All but one are males. By itself, this statistical argument does not prove discrimination. Statistically speaking, the average murderer is mostly black, poor, male.

Bryant Huff, district attorney for Gwinnett County north of Atlanta, successful prosecutor in four death-sentence verdicts, says it is a matter of common sense.

"If you've got six times as many blacks committing capital felonies as whites, is it discriminatory that six times as many blacks are on Death Row? I'm not saying it's six times more, but you get the point. Now, does the millionaire kid have to get out and rob? No. But we don't contend that the poor kids have to get out and rob. How many poor kids don't get out and rob, but work their butts off to make their money?"

As it happens, all of Huff's convictions are of white men. His office wall is covered with photographs of murder gore: two men lying in a bloody drainage ditch, a high school principal with his forehead split asunder, brains disgorging. Huff wears a little lapel pin to show where he stands—a golden hangman's noose suspended from a tree limb.

"Now that doesn't symbolize lynching," Huff explains. "That symbolizes I support capital punishment."

Popular Opinion Supports Capital Punishment

So do most Americans, it seems, including most Georgians. When the Supreme Court voided all existing death-penalty laws back in 1972 on the grounds that they were arbitrarily applied, most state legislatures rushed to enact new ones. At present, according to the Gallup Poll, 65 per cent of the public favors the death penalty for murder, the strongest support since 1953.

The high water mark for abolition was 1966, when 47 per cent of the public opposed executions and 42 per cent supported them. Everyone knows what has happened in the intervening 10 years: crime in America soared, especially murder. In 1966, there were 10,980 homicides recorded; last year there were 20,510. Bryant Huff has the folks on his side and Millard Farmer knows it.

The abolitionist argument, if it is to prevail, will have to rely on more complicated proof, evidence of random justice so strong it can convert public opinion or override it in court. Here are some examples of recent murder convictions and their sentences, all taken from Georgia court records:

- Paul Edwards and Jill Shaw were lovers in suburban DeKalb County and wanted to eliminate Edwards' wife. With his help, Shaw stabbed her in the face six times, a successful murder. Rebecca Machetti and her husband,

Anthony, were living in Florida when a man named John Mauree shot and killed Mrs. Machetti's first husband in Macon, Ga. Mauree pleaded guilty to the murder, but said the Machettis put him up to it.

Who shall die? Of all these, only the Machettis.

- Andrew Thomas Massey, a 30-year-old white man, held up a 7-Eleven store in DeKalb County and blew off the head of the woman clerk. Jesse Pulliam, a 24-year-old black man, held up a white taxi driver in rural Troup County, in western Georgia, shot the man in the neck and killed him.

Massey is doing 15 years for voluntary manslaughter, perhaps because the store clerk he killed happened to be his wife. Pulliam is going to be executed.

- Linda Porter robbed a woman at a Dalton, Ga., motel, stabbing her 76 times, fatally, assisted in the getaway by her boyfriend, L.B. Lawless. Guy Mason shot his girlfriend during a fight in Milledgeville.

Mason, convicted of a previous homicide, dies. Porter gets life in prison. Lawless gets nothing—he was given immunity in exchange for testifying against his girlfriend.

If the point is still not clear, consider the case of Edward Ward, a black man who was fired from his job in suburban Atlanta and decided to get even. He returned with a machete, chopped a woman's head off, hacked a man to death.

The first time Ward was tried for murder, he got life. The verdict was set aside on appeal. At the second trial, Ward got a hung jury, unable to reach a verdict. At the third trial, he got death.

This Death Penalty Still Seems Unfair

If this sounds vaguely like a lottery wheel, a cynical lawyer like Millard Farmer, who has never lost a client to the death penalty, insists that the sentencing is less fair than random chance would be. Certain factors unbalance the wheel, according to Farmer, who picks the most likely candidates for death to represent as clients.

"The kind of case that gets a guilty plea in exchange for a life sentence is the kind of case where the defendant has a good or excellent lawyer," Farmer said. "He's got to be ready to go all out. One of the things a DA has to think about is what kind of fight he's in. If he sees a little old guy he can whip in two days, he's going to whip him. It's that simple."

More specifically, Farmer said, the death sentence follows particular defendants in particular places with particular victims. "The best cases involve a person who's been arrested many times, with public sentiment against him, a small town [where] a favorite son has been murdered, a target defendant who is black or poor or someone who has moved into town recently. It's not only the race of the defendant but the race of the victim—it's usually black-on-white."

In Georgia, for instance, only 6 of the 66 people facing execution are from Atlanta—yet Atlanta produced about one-fourth of the state's homicides. Small towns and bedroom suburbs produce the stiffer sentences.

No statistics on victims seem to be available for Georgia murders, but a national study of 1974–1975 death sentences handed down under the new "guided discretion" laws, including Georgia's, found that 92 per cent of the cases involved white victims. Only 7 per cent were black-on-black murders. Only 1 per cent involved white-on-black.

Surveying Georgia cases, indeed, suggests some crude rules for avoiding the death sentence in that state: If you must murder, do it in Atlanta. Don't murder a white person. Murder someone in your own family, your wife or child, or, better still, your girl friend's child. Do not confess (it only tightens the case against you, which increases the chance that the DA may go for the death penalty). Hire a lawyer who will exhaust every defense tactic, file every conceivable motion, tie up the prosecution with a lengthy and expensive trial. If you are poor, call Millard Farmer, who will do the same thing.

Mercy

But Bryant Huff, the Gwinnett County prosecutor, has another name for all these examples of unevenness in the law. He calls it "mercy."

"If I execute my discretion and do not prosecute someone who might ought to get death," Huff insisted, "that guy cannot complain—he got the benefit of mercy. The Supreme Court should concern itself only with those who get the death penalty and whether they fall within the law. If they do, then the law is not discriminatory. It's discriminatory only if a person is included in the death penalty category for discriminatory reasons. He has no reason to complain because these other people received mercy."

Huff has what he regards as the clincher argument—the reason why it will be very difficult to sell Millard Farmer's case to the courts, even if it is exhaustively documented. To conclude that the death penalty is handed out in discriminatory ways is to ask how fairly *all* forms of punishment are administered to the guilty.

"It would be impossible to send anybody to jail," Huff said, confident that the Supreme Court agrees with him.

> "There is the feeling recognized by courts and juries that there are certain crimes so evil that society is justified in using the ultimate sanction against the perpetrators of them."

The Court Ruled Correctly in *Gregg*

National Review

In this 1976 editorial published shortly after the Supreme Court's ruling in Gregg v. Georgia, *the conservative newsmagazine* National Review *celebrated the fact that capital punishment was once again acceptable in the American legal system. In reaching this decision,* National Review *concluded, the Supreme Court appropriately recognized the suffering of crime victims and the truly evil nature of certain crimes. In response to concerns from death penalty opponents, the magazine concluded by quoting an African American Illinois state senator, who pointed out that while most of those who would be put to death were poor persons of color, most of the victims of those who would be put to death were also poor persons of color.* National Review, *which was founded in 1955 by William F. Buckley Jr., was perhaps the most important conservative publication in the United States during the second half of the twentieth century.*

In *Gregg v. Georgia*, the Supreme Court has ruled, 7 to 2, that the death penalty—at least for murder—is not inherently a cruel or unusual punishment but rather a constitu-

National Review, "Not Cruel; No Longer Unusual," July 20, 1976. Copyright © 1976 by National Review, Inc., 215 Lexington Avenue, New York, NY 10016. Reproduced by permission.

tionally acceptable one, providing that it is meted out only after a careful inquiry into the character of the criminal and the circumstances of his crime. The Court's decision settles the principal question at issue since 1963, when Justice Arthur Goldberg wrote a memorandum to his fellow Justices urging them to scrutinize the relationship between the "supreme penalty" and the Constitution, and thereby sparked an assault against the imposition of that penalty. It is because of that assault that no convicted criminal has been executed in this country for the past nine years—because of it too that the Supreme Court ruled in 1972 in *Furman v. Georgia* that the death penalty, as it was then meted out by the states, did indeed constitute "cruel and unusual punishment," imposed, in the Court's words, "in an arbitrary or capricious manner."

The Ultimate Sanction

The Court ruled as it did in *Gregg* because 35 states, including Georgia, have reworked their laws to conform with *Furman*. The Court in *Gregg* relied heavily upon the argument that the state legislatures, by putting legal provisions for the death penalty on their books, may fairly be said to have established capital punishment as a reflection of contemporary standards of decency.

Gregg v. Georgia leaves some 600 death-row inmates in the United States, of whom perhaps half have been sentenced according to laws now invalidated by the Court's ruling. But no doubt it will be several months before there is an execution. The Attorney General of Texas—one of the three states whose laws the Court specifically upheld—says: "We are not going to see wholesale executions in Texas. We are not going to see any immediate executions." Although Arthur Goldberg has called the decision "one of the worst decisions since the *Dred Scott* opinion ... just terrible," there is the feeling recognized by courts and juries that there are certain crimes so evil that society is justified in using the ultimate sanction against the perpetrators of them. In the Texas case, for instance, Jerry Lane Jurek was convicted of the murder of a ten-year-old girl who refused his sexual advances, whom he strangled, and whose body he tossed in a river. To quote a black state senator from Illinois: "I realize that most of those who would face the death penalty are poor and black and friendless. I also realize that most of their victims are poor and black and friendless and dead."

> "A close inspection of who our courts actually sentence to death reveals that the promise of Gregg has not been fulfilled."

History Shows That *Gregg* Was a Mistake

Michael L. Radelet

In 2001, on the twenty-fifth anniversary of Gregg v. Georgia, *then-University of Florida professor Michael L. Radelet analyzed the* Gregg *decision for Amnesty International USA. The following selection is excerpted from his analysis. Pointing out that the decision had "dashed the hopes" of many Americans who had rejoiced at the 1972* Furman v. Georgia *decision suspending the death penalty, Radelet argued that the* Gregg *decision was seriously flawed. Radelet explained that since the Court's decision in* Gregg, *which held that states could impose the death penalty if they created appropriate statutes to guide judges and juries in sentencing convicts, public opinion in the United States had increasingly turned against capital punishment. More importantly, Radelet added, the death penalty seemed increasingly to be applied in a biased fashion against African Americans, suggesting that the post-*Furman *statutes were not sufficient to prevent racial discrimination in deciding who should be put to death. Radelet, a professor of sociology at the University of Colorado at Boulder, is a renowned expert on (and opponent of) capital punishment who has authored numerous publications on the death penalty and has testified as an expert witness in over sixty trials.*

Michael L. Radelet, *The Death Penalty In America: Twenty-five Years After* Gregg v. Georgia. New York: Amnesty International USA, 2001. Copyright © 2001 by Amnesty International USA. Reproduced by permission.

The Death Penalty

On July 2, 1976, the U.S. Supreme Court decided *Gregg v. Georgia* and several companion cases, thereby reinstituting the death penalty in the United States. These decisions dashed the hopes of many Americans who, at the time, believed the United States had seen its last execution. The promise of permanent abolition seemed especially attainable just four years earlier, when, in *Furman v. Georgia*, the Court had (in effect) abolished all existing death penalty statutes in the nation. . . .

Furman condemned the arbitrary and capricious application of the death penalty; *Gregg* held that a properly written statute could bridle and guide the discretion used to make death penalty decisions. Anthony Amsterdam [a law professor who volunteered his assistance to both Furman and Gregg] argued in his brief in *Gregg* that "the changes in the Georgia sentencing procedure are only cosmetic, that the arbitrariness and capriciousness condemned by *Furman* continue to exist in Georgia." A fair-minded observer might well argue that the four years between the two cases did not provide enough data to tell with constitutional assurance whether the new statutes did yield only "cosmetic" changes or whether they really did improve things. Now, 25 years later, we are in a better position to judge. By briefly examining issues of evolving standards of human decency, the penological justifications for death, and the issues of racial bias and arbitrariness in death sentencing, we can focus some of the debate over which of the two decisions was better.

Evolving Standards of Decency

Gregg found that the death penalty did not offend "the evolving standards of decency which mark the progress of a maturing society." While that may be true of the death penalty as it exists on the statute books, what more can we learn about the death penalty by looking at how it has actually been applied over the past two dozen years? We need to look at these facts because support for the death penalty in the abstract is a very different question from support for the death penalty as it is actually applied.

The death penalty clearly violates the evolving moral standards of most other countries with whom the United States shares its human rights commitments, and it clearly violates the evolving moral standards of most religious organizations. Worldwide, more and more countries over the past 25 years have abolished the death penalty, to the point where today the majority of countries in the world have entirely banned the executioner. Virtually all western democracies are abolitionist jurisdictions; in 1999, 85 percent of all judicial executions (those imposed by courts under law) were carried out in just five countries: China, Iran, Saudi Arabia, the Democratic Republic of the Congo, and the United States. Almost all the major religious denominations in the nation have also found the death penalty to violate their evolving moral standards. The lack of legal protections in many American jurisdictions for juveniles and the mentally disabled has also raised worldwide concerns. And, with over seven dozen inmates released from America's death rows since the time of *Furman* because of doubts about their guilt, one can only speculate how many equally innocent defendants were not so lucky and instead were wrongfully put to death. Does not the increasing recognition of the inevitability of executing the innocent offend evolving moral standards?

Furthermore, evidence from recent public opinion polls suggests that more and more Americans are turning away from the death penalty, also indicating a possible change in evolving moral standards. In a poll taken in early 2000, the Gallup Organization found that only 52 percent of Americans supported capital punishment given an alternative of life-without-parole, and that overall support for the death penalty was at its lowest level in 19 years. An NBC/Wall Street Journal poll, taken in July 2000, found that 63 percent of the American public favored an immediate moratorium on executions. In January 2000 Illinois governor George Ryan imposed a moratorium on executions in his state. In 1999 the Nebraska legislature passed legislation calling for a moratorium and in 2000 the New Hampshire legislature voted to abolish the death penalty; while the governors in both states vetoed these bills, they do show that support for the death penalty may have peaked.

Arbitrariness and Racial Bias

The statutes approved in the *Gregg* decision, in effect, permitted the death penalty for only a small proportion of those convicted of homicide. In the past twenty-five years, only about 2 or 3 percent of those convicted of homicide have been sentenced to death. If the laws operated as they should, only the very worst of those convicted killers, and those and only those convicted of the most aggravated murders, would end up on death row. But a close inspection of who our courts actually sentence to death reveals that the promise of *Gregg* has not been fulfilled.

Arbitrariness occurs when there is no reliable basis for distinguishing between those who are sentenced to death and those who are not. This issue was raised by Justice [Potter] Stewart in *Furman*, when he argued that death sentences were being imposed in a way as capricious as being struck by lightning. Today we have a death penalty system where many scholars have found that the capriciousness condemned in *Furman* still exists. Whether one lives or dies seems more a function of the quality of the defendant's legal counsel or pure luck than any of the relevant characteristics of the crime or the offender's prior record.

A related problem related to arbitrariness is that distinctions can indeed be made between those sentenced to death and others sentenced to prison terms, but on the basis of legally irrelevant factors. Chief among them is race.

Clearly, a step in the right direction in the past three decades was the Supreme Court's decision in *Coker* [*v. Georgia*] (1977), the case in which the death penalty was prohibited for those convicted of rape. But aside from that, there has been virtually no progress in reducing the racial disparities of death row populations. Compare, for example, the racial characteristics of those executed for murder from 1930 to 1967 to the racial characteristics of those on death row today:

	Executed for Murder, 1930–67	On Death Row 7/1/00
White	1,664 (.499)	1,701 (.462)
Black or Other	1,670 (.501)	1,981 (.538)
Total	3,334	3,682

So, the proportion of non-whites among those executed for murder between 1930 and 1967 was 50 percent; today the non-white population of those on death row *has risen* to 53.8 percent. In short, if we focus attention on death sentences for murder, we can see that the racial disparities in today's death sentencing are even worse than in the years before *Furman*.

Penological Justifications: Retribution and Deterrence

If one accepts the principle annunciated in *Gregg* that retribution is a constitutionally permissible justification for the death penalty, its legitimacy rests on the idea that only the worst of all murders and murderers are punished by death. That is, retribution contains within it a proportionality argument—we should have the most severe punishments for the most severe crimes. To the degree that the administration of the death penalty is characterized by the arbitrariness and racial bias noted above, its retributive justification diminishes. Furthermore, since *Gregg* more and more states have passed statutes providing for "Life Without Parole" for those not sentenced to death, giving a criminal justice focused on retribution a non-lethal alternative.

Justice Stewart's plurality opinion in *Gregg* also justified the death penalty on deterrent grounds. They characterized the evidence of deterrence as "inconclusive," but then suggest that "[t]here are carefully contemplated murders . . . where the possible penalty of death may well enter into the cold calculus that precedes the decision to act." Since 1976 scores of projects have examined the deterrence issue, and a 1996 survey of America's top criminologists found that some 85% of the experts agreed that the empirical research on deterrence has shown that the death penalty never has been, is not, and never could be superior to long prison sentences as a deterrent to criminal violence.

Hence, the Court's 1976 justifications for the death penalty can and should be revisited.

The 25th anniversary of the *Gregg* decision presents us with an invitation to reexamine it, compare it to the *Furman* decision, and evaluate which was the better. Amnesty International strongly believes that in *Furman*, the Court was right.

CHAPTER 3

Forbidding the Execution of the Mentally Retarded

Chapter Preface

Case Overview: *Atkins v. Virginia* (2002)

In *Atkins v. Virginia* (2002), reversing its 1989 *Penry v. Lynaugh* decision, the U.S. Supreme Court ruled in a 6-3 decision that execution of the mentally retarded violates the Eighth Amendment prohibition against cruel and unusual punishment. The *Atkins* ruling, which was one of several in the late 1990s and early 2000s that substantially limited use of the death penalty, raised significant problems because states now needed to determine which offenders were mentally retarded. In the wake of the *Atkins* ruling, some experts argued that the decision to impose the death penalty now often depended on subjective evaluations of mental acuity.

In August 1996 Daryl Atkins and an accomplice kidnapped, robbed, and executed a young air force airman. Atkins was convicted and sentenced to death in Virginia on the strength of two aggravating circumstances ("future dangerousness" and "vileness of the offense"). During the penalty phase a defense expert testified that Atkins was mentally retarded, while a prosecution expert testified that Atkins was of normal intelligence. Responding to the continuing national debate over whether to execute the mentally retarded, the Court agreed to consider Atkins's appeal.

Writing for the majority, Justice John Paul Stevens cited national opinion data, international opinion, and the actions of numerous state legislatures—all of which, he maintained, demonstrated an "emerging national consensus" against capital punishment for the mentally retarded. Moreover, Stevens argued, while mentally retarded persons are often competent to stand trial, they have diminished capacities to understand and to control impulses, and therefore their personal culpability is at least partially diminished. Execution of the mentally retarded, Stevens concluded, must be considered cruel and unusual.

In a strongly worded and acerbic dissent, Justice Antonin Scalia argued that the Court had erred in identifying an "emerging national consensus" and that objective data clearly demonstrated that no such consensus had yet been reached. The Court's decision, Scalia concluded, was based more on the individual prejudices of the justices than on an intelligent reading of the law. This ruling, he added, would have the effect of turning "the process of capital trial into a game" as offenders sought to pretend that they were mentally retarded. Scalia was joined in his decision by Justice Clarence Thomas and Chief Justice William Rehnquist, who also wrote a separate opinion arguing that the Court had erred seriously in relying on "foreign laws, the views of professional and religious organizations, and opinion polls." In attempting to ascertain contemporary American standards of decency, Rehnquist concluded, the Court should look only to the results of state legislation and jury decisions.

The *Atkins* ruling, which some critics described as a ruling that people can be "too stupid to die," raises serious questions about the nature of mental retardation, the use of intelligence testing, and even the nature of criminal culpability. While Justice Scalia's fear that offenders would attempt to fake mental retardation has not been realized, a serious and immediate problem remains how to determine whether offenders are in fact mentally retarded. In *Atkins* the Court decided to leave it to the individual states to define "mental retardation," and the result is that different states have different (and sometimes conflicting) definitions. In Virginia, where Atkins had committed his murder, a mentally retarded offender is one with an IQ below seventy who has "significant limitations in adaptive behavior" that were evident before age eighteen. While Atkins did not take an IQ test until after he had turned eighteen, on the four tests he later took he scored fifty-nine, sixty-seven, seventy-four, and seventy-six, respectively (below seventy is typically considered retarded). A new jury, which was impaneled in 2005, heard evidence from both the prosecution and the defense about Atkins's background and personal history and ultimately concluded that Atkins was not in fact mentally retarded; ironically, the murderer whose case set a new national precedent in restricting the death penalty was thus once again himself sentenced to die.

> "Mentally retarded defendants in the aggregate face a special risk of wrongful execution."

Majority Opinion: Executing the Mentally Retarded Is Excessive Punishment

John Paul Stevens

In this excerpt from the Supreme Court's majority opinion in Atkins v. Virginia, *Justice John Paul Stevens concluded that the execution of the mentally retarded violated the Eighth Amendment prohibitions against cruel and unusual punishment. One element in determining whether a punishment is cruel and unusual, Stevens noted, is whether it violates society's ever-changing standards of decency. Citing numerous recent state laws and amicus briefs filed by religious groups, civil rights organizations, and even the European Union, Stevens argued that America was witnessing the emergence of a new national consensus against the execution of the mentally retarded. Noting that the mentally retarded act more on impulse than with "cold calculation," Stevens concluded that executing the retarded would not deter other mentally retarded criminals. In addition, because the mentally retarded are less able than other defendants to defend themselves, Stevens noted, they are more likely to be wrongfully convicted and executed. Accordingly, citing "evolving standards of decency" in the United States, Stevens concluded that the execution of the mentally retarded was unconstitutional. Stevens was joined in this opinion by Justices Sandra Day O'Connor,*

John Paul Stevens, majority opinion, *Atkins v. Virginia*, U.S. Supreme Court, June 20, 2002.

Ruth Bader Ginsburg, David Souter, Anthony M. Kennedy, and Stephen Breyer. Stevens was appointed to the Supreme Court by President Gerald Ford in December 1975 and was confirmed by the Senate the following year.

Those mentally retarded persons who meet the law's requirements for criminal responsibility should be tried and punished when they commit crimes. Because of their disabilities in areas of reasoning, judgment, and control of their impulses, however, they do not act with the level of moral culpability that characterizes the most serious adult criminal conduct. Moreover, their impairments can jeopardize the reliability and fairness of capital proceedings against mentally retarded defendants. . . .

Prohibiting Excessive Punishment

The Eighth Amendment succinctly prohibits "excessive" sanctions. It provides: "Excessive bail shall not be required, nor excessive fines imposed, nor cruel and unusual punishments inflicted." In *Weems v. United States* (1910), we held that a punishment of 12 years jailed in irons at hard and painful labor for the crime of falsifying records was excessive. We explained "that it is a precept of justice that punishment for crime should be graduated and proportioned to the offense" . . .

As Chief Justice [Earl] Warren explained in his opinion in *Trop v. Dulles* (1958): "The basic concept underlying the Eighth Amendment is nothing less than the dignity of man. . . . The Amendment must draw its meaning from the evolving standards of decency that mark the progress of a maturing society." . . .

Standards of Decency Are Changing

The parties have not called our attention to any state legislative consideration of the suitability of imposing the death penalty on mentally retarded offenders prior to 1986. In that year, the public reaction to the execution of a mentally retarded murderer in Georgia apparently led to the enactment of the first state statute prohibiting such executions. In 1988, when Congress enacted legislation reinstating the federal death penalty, it expressly provided that a "sentence of death shall not be carried out upon a person who is mentally retarded." In 1989, Maryland enacted a similar prohibition. It was in that year that we decided *Penry*, and concluded that those two state enactments, "even when added to the 14 States that have rejected capital punishment completely, do not provide sufficient evidence at present of a national consensus."

Much has changed since then. Responding to the national attention received by the Bowden execution and our decision in *Penry*, state legislatures across the country began to address the issue. In 1990 Kentucky and Tennessee enacted statutes similar to those in Georgia and Maryland, as did New Mexico in 1991, and Arkansas, Colorado, Washington, Indiana, and Kansas in 1993 and 1994. In 1995, when New York reinstated its death penalty, it emulated the Federal Government by expressly exempting the mentally retarded. Nebraska followed suit in 1998. There appear to have been no similar enactments during the next two years, but in 2000 and 2001 six more States—South Dakota, Arizona, Connecticut, Florida, Missouri, and North Carolina—joined the procession. The Texas Legislature unanimously adopted a similar bill, and bills have passed at least one house in other States, including Virginia and Nevada.

It is not so much the number of these States that is significant, but the consistency of the direction of change. Given the well-known fact that anticrime legislation is far more popular than legislation providing protections for persons guilty of violent crime, the large number of States prohibiting the execution of mentally retarded persons (and the complete absence of States passing legislation reinstating the power to conduct such executions) provides powerful evidence that today our society views mentally retarded offenders as categorically less culpable than the average criminal. The evidence carries even greater force when it is noted that the legislatures that have addressed the issue have voted overwhelmingly in favor of the prohibition. Moreover, even in those States that allow the execution of mentally retarded offenders, the practice is uncommon. Some States, for example New Hampshire and New Jersey, continue to authorize executions, but none have been carried out in decades. Thus there is little need to pursue legislation barring the execution of the mentally retarded in those States. And it appears that even among those States that regularly execute offenders and that have no prohibition with regard to the mentally retarded, only five have executed offenders possessing a known IQ less than 70 since we decided *Penry*. The practice, therefore, has become truly unusual, and it is fair to say that a national consensus has developed against it. . . .

The Retarded Share Behavioral Characteristics

This consensus unquestionably reflects widespread judgment about the relative culpability of mentally retarded offenders, and the relationship between mental retardation and the penological purposes served by the death penalty. Additionally, it suggests that some characteristics of mental retardation undermine the strength of the procedural protections that our capital jurisprudence steadfastly guards.

. . . Clinical definitions of mental retardation require not only subaverage intellectual functioning, but also significant limitations in adaptive skills such as communication, self-care, and self-direction that became manifest before age 18. Mentally retarded persons frequently know the difference between right and wrong and are competent to stand trial. Because of their impairments, however, by definition they have dimin-

Daryl Atkins's 2002 case led the Supreme Court to rule that execution of the mentally retarded violated the Eighth Amendment's prohibitions against cruel and unusual punishment. AP/Wide World Photos

ished capacities to understand and process information, to communicate, to abstract from mistakes and learn from experience, to engage in logical reasoning, to control impulses, and to understand the reactions of others. There is no evidence that they are more likely to engage in criminal conduct than others, but there is abundant evidence that they often act on impulse rather than pursuant to a premeditated plan, and that in group settings they are followers rather than leaders. Their deficiencies do not warrant an exemption from criminal sanctions, but they do diminish their personal culpability.

Measuring Retribution and Deterrence

In light of these deficiencies, our death penalty jurisprudence provides two reasons consistent with the legislative consensus that the mentally retarded should be categorically excluded from execution. First, there is a serious question as to whether either justification that we have recognized as a basis for the death penalty applies to mentally retarded offenders. *Gregg v. Georgia* (1976) identified "retribution and deterrence of capital crimes by prospective offenders" as the social purposes served by the death penalty. Unless the imposition of the death penalty on a mentally retarded person "measurably contributes to one or both of these goals, it 'is nothing more than the purposeless and needless imposition of pain and suffering,' and hence an unconstitutional punishment" [*Enmund v. Florida* (1982)].

With respect to retribution—the interest in seeing that the offender gets his "just deserts"—the severity of the appropriate punishment necessarily depends on the culpability of the offender. Since *Gregg*, our jurisprudence has consistently confined the imposition of the death penalty to a narrow category of the most serious crimes. For example, in *Godfrey v. Georgia* (1980) we set aside a death sentence because the petitioner's crimes did not reflect "a consciousness materially more 'depraved' than that of any person guilty of murder." If the culpability of the average murderer is insufficient to justify the most extreme sanction available to the State, the lesser culpability of the mentally retarded offender surely does not merit that form of retribution. Thus, pursuant to our narrowing jurisprudence, which seeks to ensure that only the most deserving of execution are put to death, an exclusion for the mentally retarded is appropriate.

With respect to deterrence—the interest in preventing capital crimes by prospective offenders—"it seems likely that 'capital punishment can serve as a deterrent only when murder is the result of premeditation and deliberation,'" *Enmund*. Exempting the mentally retarded from that punishment will not affect the "cold calculus that precedes the decision" of other potential murderers. Indeed, that sort of calculus is at the opposite end of the spectrum from behavior of mentally retarded offenders. The theory of deterrence in capital sentencing is predicated upon the notion that the increased severity of the punishment will inhibit criminal actors from carrying out murderous conduct. Yet it is the same cognitive and behavioral impairments that make these defendants less morally culpable—for example, the diminished ability to understand and process information, to learn from experience, to engage in logical reasoning, or to control impulses—that also make it less likely that they can process the information of the possibility of execution as a penalty and, as a result, control their conduct based upon that information. Nor will exempting the mentally retarded from execution lessen the deterrent effect of the death penalty with respect to offenders who are not mentally retarded. Such individuals are unprotected by the exemption and will continue to face the threat of execution. Thus, executing the mentally retarded will not measurably further the goal of deterrence.

The Retarded Make Poor Witnesses

The reduced capacity of mentally retarded offenders provides a second justification for a categorical rule making such offenders ineligible for the death penalty. The risk "that the death penalty will be imposed in spite of factors which may call for a less severe penalty" [*Lockett v. Ohio* (1978)] is enhanced, not only by the possibility of false confessions, but also by the lesser ability of mentally retarded defendants to make a persuasive showing of mitigation in the face of prosecutorial evidence of one or more aggravating factors. Mentally retarded defendants may be less able to give meaningful assistance to their counsel and are typically poor witnesses, and their demeanor may create an unwarranted impression of lack of remorse for their crimes. As *Penry* demonstrated, moreover, reliance on mental retardation as a mitigating factor can be a two-edged sword that may enhance the likelihood that the aggravating factor of future dangerousness will be found by the jury. Mentally retarded defendants in the aggregate face a special risk of wrongful execution.

Our independent evaluation of the issue reveals no reason to disagree with the judgment of "the legislatures that have recently addressed the matter" and concluded that death is not a suitable punishment for a mentally retarded criminal. We are not persuaded that the execution of mentally retarded criminals will measurably advance the deterrent or the retributive purpose of the death penalty. Construing and applying the Eighth Amendment in the light of our "evolving standards of decency," we therefore conclude that such punishment is excessive and that the Constitution "places a substantive restriction on the State's power to take the life" of a mentally retarded offender. *Ford.*

The judgment of the Virginia Supreme Court is reversed and the case is remanded for further proceedings not inconsistent with this opinion.

It is so ordered.

> "Seldom has an opinion of this Court rested so obviously upon nothing but the personal views of its members."

Dissenting Opinion: Executing the Mentally Retarded Is Not Unconstitutional

Antonin Scalia

In this excerpt from his acerbic dissent in Atkins v. Virginia *(in which he was joined by Chief Justice William Rehnquist and Justice Clarence Thomas), Justice Antonin Scalia argued that the Court's majority opinion was logically flawed and was based more on personal opinion than on any matter of law. What his colleagues viewed as a clear emerging national consensus against the execution of the mentally retarded, he argued, was in fact a confused and indeterminate national debate about whether such executions were appropriate. Viewing the* Atkins *ruling as part of a series of decisions limiting use of the death penalty, Scalia criticized the Court for interfering in matters that should be left to state legislatures. Rather than forbidding execution of the mentally retarded, he added, courts should allow juries to consider a defendant's mental acuity as one factor in deciding appropriate punishment. Scalia, consistently one of the most conservative members of the Supreme Court, was appointed to the Court in 1986 by President Ronald Reagan.*

Today's decision is the pinnacle of our Eighth Amendment death-is-different jurisprudence. Not only does it, like all of that jurisprudence, find no support in the text or history of

Antonin Scalia, dissenting opinion, *Atkins v. Virginia*, U.S. Supreme Court, June 20, 2002.

the Eighth Amendment; it does not even have support in current social attitudes regarding the conditions that render an otherwise just death penalty inappropriate. Seldom has an opinion of this Court rested so obviously upon nothing but the personal views of its members. . . .

Historically the Retarded Were Not Specially Protected

Under our Eighth Amendment jurisprudence, a punishment is "cruel and unusual" if it falls within one of two categories: "those modes or acts of punishment that had been considered cruel and unusual at the time that the Bill of Rights was adopted" [*Ford v. Wainwright* (1986)], and modes of punishment that are inconsistent with modern "standards of decency," as evinced by objective indicia, the most important of which is "legislation enacted by the country's legislatures," *Penry v. Lynaugh* (1989).

The Court makes no pretense that execution of the mildly mentally retarded would have been considered "cruel and unusual" in 1791. . . .

The Court is left to argue, therefore, that execution of the mildly retarded is inconsistent with the "evolving standards of decency that mark the progress of a maturing society." *Trop v. Dulles* (1958) (plurality opinion) (Warren, C.J.). Before today, our opinions consistently emphasized that Eighth Amendment judgments regarding the existence of social "standards" "should be informed by objective factors to the maximum possible extent" and "should not be, or appear to be, merely the subjective views of individual Justices." *Coker v. Georgia* (1977) (plurality opinion). "First" among these objective factors are the "statutes passed by society's elected representatives," [*Stanford v. Kentucky* (1989)]; because it "will rarely if ever be the case that the Members of this Court will have a better sense of the evolution in views of the American people than do their elected representatives," *Thompson* (Scalia, J., dissenting).

There Is No National Consensus

The Court pays lipservice to these precedents as it miraculously extracts a "national consensus" forbidding execution of the mentally retarded from the fact that 18 States—less than *half* (47%) of the 38 States that permit capital punishment (for whom the issue exists)—have very recently enacted legislation barring execution of the mentally retarded. Even that 47% figure is a distorted one. If one is to say, as the Court does today, that *all* executions of the mentally retarded are so morally repugnant as to violate our national "standards of decency," surely the "consensus" it points to must be one that has set its righteous face against *all* such executions. Not 18 States, but only seven—18% of death penalty jurisdictions—have legislation of that scope. Eleven of those that the Court counts enacted statutes prohibiting execution of mentally retarded defendants *convicted after, or convicted of crimes committed after, the effective date* of the legislation, those already on death row, or consigned there before the statute's effective date, or even (in those States using the date of the crime as the criterion of retroactivity) tried in the future for murders committed many years ago, could be put to death. That is not a statement of absolute moral repugnance, but one of current preference between two tolerable approaches. Two of these States permit execution of the mentally retarded in other situations as well: Kansas apparently permits execution of all except the *severely* mentally retarded; New York permits execution of the mentally retarded who commit murder in a correctional facility.

But let us accept, for the sake of argument, the Court's faulty count. That bare number of States alone—*18*—should be enough to convince any reasonable person that no "national consensus" exists. How is it possible that agreement among 47% of the death penalty jurisdictions amounts to "consensus" ? Our prior cases have generally required a much higher degree of agreement before finding a punishment cruel and unusual on "evolving standards" grounds. . . .

Moreover, a major factor that the Court entirely disregards is that the legislation of all 18 States it relies on is still in its infancy. The oldest of the statutes is only 14 years old; five were enacted last year; over half were enacted within the past eight years. Few, if any, of the States have had sufficient experience with these laws to know whether they are sensible in the long term. It is "myopic to base sweeping constitutional principles upon the narrow experience of [a few] years." *Coker* (Burger, C. J., dissenting).

Evidence of Changing Standards Is Misleading

The Court attempts to bolster its embarrassingly feeble evidence of "consensus" with the following: "It is not so much the number of these States that is significant, but the *consistency* of the direction of change." (emphasis added). But in what *other* direction *could we possibly* see change? Given that 14 years ago *all* the death penalty statutes included the mentally retarded, *any* change (except precipitate undoing of what had just been done) was *bound to be* in the one direction the Court finds significant enough to overcome the lack of real consensus. That is to say, to be accurate the Court's "*consistency* -of-the-direction-of-change" point should be recast into the following unimpressive observation: "No State has yet undone its exemption of the mentally retarded, one for as long as 14 whole years." In any event, reliance upon "trends," even those of much longer duration than a mere 14 years, is a perilous basis for constitutional adjudication. . . .

But the Prize for the Court's Most Feeble Effort to fabricate "national consensus" must go to its appeal (deservedly relegated to a footnote) to the views of assorted professional and religious organizations, members of the so-called "world community," and respondents to opinion polls. I agree with the Chief Justice (dissenting opinion), that the views of professional and religious organizations and the results of opinion polls are irrelevant. Equally irrelevant are the practices of the "world community," whose notions of justice are (thankfully) not always those of our people. "We must never forget that it is a Constitution for the United States of America that we are expounding. . . . [W]here there is not first a settled consensus among our own people, the views of other nations, however enlightened the Justices of this Court may think them to be, cannot be imposed upon Americans through the Constitution." *Thompson* (Scalia, J., dissenting).

Deciding on Personal Opinion

Beyond the empty talk of a "national consensus," the Court gives us a brief glimpse of what really underlies today's decision: pretension to a power confined *neither* by the moral sentiments originally enshrined in the Eighth Amendment (its original meaning) *nor even* by the current moral sentiments of the American people. "'[T]he Constitution,'" the Court says, "contemplates that in the end *our own judgment* will be brought to bear on the question of the acceptability of the death penalty under the Eighth Amendment.'" (quoting *Coker*) (emphasis added). (The unexpressed reason for this unexpressed "contemplation" of the Constitution is presumably that really good lawyers have moral sentiments superior to those of the common herd, whether in 1791 or today.) The arrogance of this assumption of power takes one's breath away. And it explains, of course, why the Court can be so cavalier about the evidence of consensus. It is just a game, after all. "[I]n the end," it is the *feelings* and *intuition* of a majority of the Justices that count—"the perceptions of decency, or of penology, or of mercy, entertained . . . by a majority of the small and unrepresentative segment of our society that sits on this Court." *Thompson* (Scalia, J., dissenting).

The genuinely operative portion of the opinion, then, is the Court's statement of the reasons why it agrees with the contrived consensus it has found, that the "diminished capacities" of the mentally retarded render the death penalty excessive. The Court's analysis rests on two fundamental assumptions: (1) that the Eighth Amendment prohibits excessive punishments, and (2) that sentencing juries or judges are unable to account properly for the "diminished capacities" of the retarded. The first assumption is wrong, as I explained at length in *Harmelin v. Michigan* (1991) (opinion of Scalia, J.). The Eighth Amendment is addressed to always-and-everywhere "cruel" punishments, such as the rack and the thumbscrew. But where the punishment is in itself permissible, "[t]he Eighth Amendment is not a ratchet, whereby a temporary consensus on leniency for a particular crime fixes a permanent constitutional maximum, disabling the States from giving effect to altered beliefs and responding to changed social conditions." The second assumption—inability of judges or juries to take proper account of mental retardation—is not only unsubstantiated, but contradicts the immemorial belief, here and in England, that they play an *indispensable* role in such matters. . . .

The Retarded Might Be Fully Culpable

Proceeding from these faulty assumptions, the Court gives two reasons why the death penalty is an excessive punishment for all mentally retarded offenders. First, the "diminished capacities" of the mentally retarded raise a "serious question" whether their execution contributes to the "social purposes" of the death penalty, viz., retribution and deterrence. (The Court conveniently ignores a third "social purpose" of the death penalty—"incapacitation of dangerous criminals and the consequent prevention of crimes that they may otherwise commit in the future," *Gregg v. Georgia* (1976) (joint opinion of Stewart, Powell, and Stevens, JJ.). But never mind; its discussion of even the other two does not bear analysis.) Retribution is not advanced, the argument goes, because the mentally retarded are *no more culpable* than the average murderer, whom we have already held lacks sufficient culpability to warrant the death penalty, see *Godfrey v. Georgia* (1980)(plurality opinion). Who says so? Is there an established correlation between mental acuity and the ability to conform one's conduct to the law in such a rudimentary matter as murder? Are the mentally retarded really more disposed (and hence more likely) to commit willfully cruel and serious crime than others? In my experience, the opposite is true: being childlike generally suggests innocence rather than brutality.

Assuming, however, that there is a direct connection between diminished intelligence and the inability to refrain from murder, what scientific analysis can possibly show that a mildly retarded individual who commits an exquisite torture-killing is "no more culpable" than the "average" murderer in a holdup-gone-wrong or a domestic dispute? Or a moderately retarded individual who commits a series of 20 exquisite torture-killings? Surely culpability, and deservedness of the most severe retribution, depends not merely (if at all) upon the mental capacity of the criminal (above the level where he is able to distinguish right from wrong) but also upon the depravity of the crime—which is precisely why this sort of question has traditionally been thought answerable not by a categorical rule of the sort the Court today imposes upon all trials, but rather by the sentencer's weighing of the circumstances (both degree of retardation and depravity of crime) in the particular case. The fact that juries continue to sentence mentally retarded offenders to death for extreme crimes shows that society's moral outrage sometimes demands execution of retarded offenders. By what principle of law, science, or logic can the Court pronounce that this is wrong? There is none. Once the Court admits (as it does) that mental retardation does not render the offender morally *blameless*, there is no basis for saying that the death penalty is *never* appropriate retribution, no matter *how* heinous the crime. As long as a mentally retarded offender knows "the difference between right and wrong," only the sentencer can assess whether his retardation reduces his culpability enough to exempt him from the death penalty for the particular murder in question. . . .

The Court throws one last factor into its grab bag of reasons why execution of the retarded is "excessive" in all cases: Mentally retarded offenders "face a special risk of wrongful execution" because they are less able "to make a persuasive showing of mitigation," "to give meaningful assistance to their counsel," and to be effective witnesses. "Special risk" is pretty flabby language (even flabbier than "less likely")—and I suppose a similar "special risk" could be said to exist for just plain stupid people, inarticulate people, even ugly people. If this unsupported claim has any substance to it (which I doubt) it might support a due process claim in all criminal prosecutions of the mentally retarded; but it is hard to see how it has anything to do with an *Eighth Amendment* claim that execution of the mentally retarded is cruel and unusual. We have never before held it to be cruel and unusual punishment to impose a sentence in violation of some *other* constitutional imperative.

Narrowing the Death Penalty

Today's opinion adds one more to the long list of substantive and procedural requirements impeding imposition of the death penalty imposed under this Court's assumed power to invent a death-is-different jurisprudence. None of those requirements existed when the Eighth Amendment was adopted, and some of them were not even supported by current moral consensus. . . . There is something to be said for popular abolition of the death penalty; there is nothing to be said for its incremental abolition by this Court. . . .

I respectfully dissent.

> "Death penalty opponents should ... be wary of a decision that threatens to add more confusion and arbitrariness to an already capricious system."

Atkins Was a Misuse of Psychiatry

Douglas Mossman

In the following selection Douglas Mossman discusses the implications of the Supreme Court's ruling in Atkins v. Virginia *and questions the Court's use of psychiatry in its decision. The majority opinion, he explains, is based on the belief that it is easy to diagnose mental retardation and to distinguish between those who are and those who are not mentally retarded. In fact, he argues, mental retardation is difficult to diagnose—in part because the very definition of "mental retardation" changes regularly. The* Atkins *ruling, he concludes, is far messier and less precise than either the Court or death penalty opponents had believed. Mossman is a professor and the director of the division of forensic psychiatry at Wright State University School of Medicine and an adjunct professor at the University of Dayton School of Law.*

The *Atkins* [*v. Virginia*] decision has been attacked by strict constructionists[1]—in his dissent Justice [Antonin] Scalia called it "nothing but the personal views of its mem-

---

1. Constructionists are legal scholars who advocate a literal interpretation of the constitution.

Douglas Mossman, "Psychiatry in the Courtroom—Psychological Testimony in Criminal Cases," *The Public Interest*, Winter 2003. Copyright © 2003 by Douglas Mossman. Reproduced by permission.

bers"—and the supporters of the death penalty. But death penalty opponents should also be wary of a decision that threatens to add more confusion and arbitrariness to an already capricious system and that seriously distorts the use of psychiatric diagnosis. To see why, one needs to consider the specifics of Daryl Renard Atkins' case, the Supreme Court majority's statements about his mental condition and diagnosis, the potential impact of these statements on the testimony of mental health experts, and the consequences for future sentencing determinations in death penalty cases.

Though Daryl Atkins was still a teenager when he committed murder, his intellectual limitations and social maladjustment had already been evident for years. Documents prepared by defense lawyers report that Atkins flunked and repeated second grade and received mainly Ds and Fs through seventh grade. School officials finally referred him for special-education testing, but he never was evaluated. He received all Fs in eighth grade, and despite not meeting requirements for entering high school, he was placed in the ninth grade, where he continued to perform poorly. He did better once he was placed in classes for "slow learners," but he still left school without graduating. By age 18—the age at which he was arrested for the murder of Eric Nesbitt—Atkins had not learned how to do laundry or cook meals for himself. . . .

When Atkins' lawyers appealed the death sentence, they did not claim that execution would be disproportionate to penalties imposed for similar crimes in Virginia. Rather, they argued that Atkins should not be sentenced to death because he was mentally retarded. A majority of the Virginia Supreme Court rejected this argument, relying on the U.S. Supreme Court's 1989 ruling in *Penry* [*v. Lynaugh*], which stated that mental retardation could be a mitigating factor but not an absolute barrier to capital punishment. Two state supreme court justices disagreed, however, arguing that retarded persons are "less culpable for their criminal acts" than other offenders because they "have substantial limitations not shared by the general population. A moral and civilized society diminishes itself if its system of justice does not afford recognition and consideration of those limitations in a meaningful way."

The Supreme Court's Ruling

Impressed by "the gravity of the concerns expressed" in the state supreme court's dissenting opinion, the U.S. Supreme Court agreed to hear Atkins' case and to revisit their 1989 decision in *Penry*. Between 1989 and 2002, the number of states with laws barring death sentences for mentally retarded persons had grown from two to eighteen, and legislatures in three other states had taken steps toward adopting such laws. Writing for the Supreme Court majority, Justice [John Paul] Stevens concluded that the passage of so many laws since the *Penry* decision showed that "much has changed" in the public's attitude about executing retarded persons. This "national consensus," which reflected "the evolving standards of decency that mark the progress of a maturing society," required the Court to change the stance it had adopted just 13 years earlier. Henceforth, a diagnosis of mental retardation would spare any murderer from the death penalty.

Footnotes in *Atkins* quote at length from diagnostic criteria that psychiatric organizations have developed to identify people with mental retardation. For example, the current diagnostic manual of the American Psychiatric Association (APA) describes mental retardation as

> significantly subaverage general intellectual functioning ... accompanied by significant limitations in adaptive functioning in at least two of the following skill areas: communication, self-care, home living, social/interpersonal skills, use of community resources, self-direction, functional academic skills, work, leisure, health, and safety ... [with] onset ... before age 18 years.

Referring to such criteria, Justice Stevens argued that "by definition," persons with mental retardation "have diminished capacities to understand and process information, to communicate, to abstract from mistakes and learn from experience, to engage in logical reasoning, to control impulses, and to understand the reactions of others." Although retarded criminals may know right from wrong, their mental deficiencies "diminish their personal culpability. Thus, pursuant to our narrowing jurisprudence, which seeks to ensure that only the most deserving of execution are put to death, an exclusion for the mentally retarded is appropriate."

Official Praise

Mental health professionals have generally praised the *Atkins* decision. The APA and the American Association on Mental Retardation (AAMR) were among the many mental health organizations that had signed on to friend-of-the-court briefs urging the Supreme Court to ban executions of retarded persons. When the *Atkins* decision was announced, Doree'n Croser, AAMR's executive director, was "deeply grateful" that the Supreme Court had stopped "this barbaric practice of killing persons who do not have the full intellectual capacity to understand the crime they committed.... This is an important day for disability advocates and for our country." Renee Binder, chair of the APA's Committee on Judicial Action, praised the decision "because it recognizes that there are objective and reliable determinations of whether an individual has mental retardation when the assessment is done by qualified professionals with substantial experience."

Binder's comment echoes points emphasized in the friend-of-the-court brief that the APA (along with the American Psychological Association and the American Academy of Psychiatry and Law) had filed with the Supreme Court. The brief argued that making psychiatric diagnosis the basis for a life-or-death legal decision would cause no scientific or practical problems. Both "incorrect diagnoses" and "unnecessary legal wrangling" could be avoided "because mental retardation can be identified using time-tested instruments and protocols with proven validity and reliability." To diagnose a person as having mental retardation, professionals must find that "three necessary criteria are all present: significant limitations in intellectual functioning, significant limitations in practical or adaptive functioning, and onset before adulthood." Psychologists and psychiatrists can make "an objective determination" about whether the accused suffers from mental retardation using established measures of intelligence and adaptive functioning, so that clinicians "undertaking separate assessments should reach the same conclusion." Yet to anyone knowledgeable about mental retardation and the methods used to diagnose it, this assertion is remarkable.

The Difficulty of Diagnosing Retardation

The "by definition" language of the *Atkins* decision suggests that persons with mental retardation form a group who are clearly distinct from nonretarded persons. In reality, mental retardation is an artificial category imposed on a spectrum of human capability. The diagnostic line that separates persons with mental retardation from those who are only well below average is a changing and arbitrary one.

One reason for this is that the criteria defining mental retardation, like most diagnostic criteria used by mental health professionals, often get revised. Over the past century, the AAMR has "updated" its definition of mental retardation 10 times. The most recent changes were published five days before the *Atkins* decision, in the tenth edition of the AAMR's official classification manual. Although psychiatric diagnoses are often revised to reflect new understandings, scientific breakthroughs, or the availability of new treatments, politics can play a role. An AAMR advertisement for Mental Retardation: Definition, Classification and Systems of Supports states unabashedly that the 2002 edition proposes a state-of-the-art method to define, classify, and support an individual with mental retardation. In view of the recent U.S. Supreme Court decision to ban execution of persons with mental retardation, the 10th edition is a timely and critical resource to the states as they strive to come up with a current and fuller definition of mental retardation.

The AAMR currently defines mental retardation as "a disability characterized by significant limitations both in intellectual functioning and in adaptive behavior as expressed in conceptual, social, and practical adaptive skills. This disability originates before the age of 18." This characterization appears reasonably close to the previously quoted definition used by the APA. Beyond this point, however, the two professional organizations begin to part in their definitions. The APA's diagnostic manual categorizes mental retardation according to its overall severity—that is, as either mild, moderate, severe, or profound. Since 1992, however, the AAMR has specifically rejected this approach. Instead, it encourages diagnosticians to examine patterns of limitations in a person's everyday functioning, and to describe the degree of support those persons need, which may be "intermittent," "limited," "extensive," or "pervasive."

If persons with mental retardation were members of a homogeneous, discrete biological or psychological category of persons, readily distinguishable from persons without mental retardation, professional organizations might have an easier time settling on clinical criteria for diagnosing the condition. There are retarded persons whose impairments make them easily identifiable: They have severe academic problems during childhood, limited communication skills, and need, even as adults, to be supervised at work or where they live. But such individuals make up only 15 percent of all retarded persons. Mildly retarded persons, who comprise the remaining 85 percent, usually develop social and work skills that enable them to minimally support themselves, though they need guidance in making complicated decisions.

The medical conditions that can cause intellectual impairment are countless. They include chromosomal defects, biochemical abnormalities, and infections that alter the brain's development before birth or during early childhood. In many cases of mild mental retardation, though, no specific medical reason for the person's limitations can be identified. Clinicians thus cannot use biological tests to decide whether a person is mentally retarded.

Testing Intelligence and Social Capability

Instead, persons with mental retardation are generally identified through tests of intelligence and social capabilities administered by specially trained professionals. When the intellectual capabilities of a large, randomly selected group of persons are measured by such tests, the result is what statisticians call a "normal distribution," often described as a "bell curve." At one end of the distribution lie geniuses, and on the other end are profoundly impaired persons; bright, average, and dull folks make up the vast majority in the middle. Intelligence testing produces a numerical result—an "intelligence quotient" or IQ score—that allows psychologists to place an individual along the spectrum of cognitive ability. Other, lesser-known tests enable psychologists and mental retardation specialists to rank individuals in terms of "adaptive" capabilities—such as communication abilities, work skills, and caring for oneself—for which the population as a whole is also continuously distributed.

IQ scores are set up so that the "mean" or average score is 100, and the "standard deviation" is 15. Approximately 95 percent of a normally distributed population lies within two standard deviations of the mean, and individuals lying outside this arbitrary statistical boundary are often deemed "abnormal." A cut-off IQ score of 70—two standard deviations below the mean score of 100—has been set as the intelligence level that separates persons with mental retardation from persons whom mental health professionals designate as having "borderline intellectual functioning." Yet such numerical definitions of mental retardation, with all the apparent precision of a mathematical formula, belie the inherent subjectivity and complexity of the problem.

Unreliable Measures

When conscientious mental health professionals interpret IQ scores and plan treatment interventions, they keep in mind that someone who scores 69 on an IQ test is practically indistinguishable from someone who scores 71, and that two persons with IQ scores of 67 and 73 have much more in common with each other than with a person who scores 88. If existing state statutes are any guide, however, legislatures and courts may lose sight of these facts when they put *Atkins* into practice. Of the 18 state statutes in effect when *Atkins* was decided, 11 made specific IQ scores part of the criteria for exempting a defendant from the death penalty. In other words, some statutes that implement *Atkins*-type barriers against execution are written such that a one-point change in a person's IQ score could make a life-or-death difference.

The availability of IQ test scores suggests that mental health professionals can offer courts objective, precise methods for deciding who is so impaired that the death penalty should be ruled out. Yet in truth the numbers that IQ tests generate are far from perfectly reliable measurements of a person's cognitive ability. Under the best conditions, IQ tests have a "measurement error" of about five points. An individual who scores, say, 68 on one administration has a 95 percent chance of scoring between 63 and 73 on subsequent administrations. More than half of the persons whose IQ results fall in the mildly retarded range receive scores of 65 to 70— that is, their scores' margin of error will include 70.

Additional uncertainty arises because, for many items, the test administrator has to decide how many points a subject's response deserves. In normal clinical use, these ambiguities do not matter a great deal. But in testing a defendant for whom a one- or two-point change in IQ score has life-and-death implications, clinicians may have a hard time being objective in interpreting a response. The net result of all these imperfections is that judges or juries will often find it difficult to decide which side of the arbitrary line—between mentally retarded and merely "dull"—a defendant falls. . . .

The Misuse and Abuse of Psychiatry

Given the high rate of serious mental illness among homicide defendants, granting psychiatric exemptions could eventually leave very few individuals eligible for the death penalty. To death penalty opponents, such a development might seem desirable. Some may be tempted to use psychiatry to eradicate the death penalty in practice. Yet whatever we may think of the morality of the death penalty, we should recognize that this strategy represents a misuse of psychiatry—one that would harm the profession as well as the legal system. The *Atkins* decision endorses the use of psychiatric categories to single out groups of citizens for distinctive legal treatment. It fails to recognize that psychiatric diagnoses are created for clinical purposes (chiefly, to guide treatment) and are periodically redefined as treatments and scientific findings reveal the errors of older categorizations. *Atkins* treats psychiatric diagnoses as fixed categories and gives them tremendous legal and social import.

Over the last several years, the U.S. Supreme Court has handed down a series of procedural and substantive requirements that give mental health professionals a considerable role in the capital punishment process. The Court has hoped that the testimony of mental health professionals would make capital sentencing fairer and more accurate. But while psychiatrists and psychologists have an important role to play in legal proceedings, letting a psychiatric diagnosis determine a defendant's sentence will not resolve the grave flaws in our nation's administration of the death penalty. Giving psychiatric diagnosis such a decisive role in capital sentencing may even compound problems with the administration of the death penalty by transforming what should be an act of moral judgment into a medical conference about a defendant's clinical disorder. Perhaps the most significant flaw in the *Atkins* decision is that it perpetuates the myth that "getting psychiatric help" will make the death penalty fairer and more palatable.

> "Even some of the public defenders eagerly making use of the Atkins decision sometimes wonder about the logic of it."

Atkins Raises Troubling Moral Questions

Margaret Talbot

In the following selection Margaret Talbot discusses various troubling implications of the Supreme Court's ruling in Atkins v. Virginia. *One problematic aspect of the decision, she argues, is that it endorses the use of IQ tests to determine intelligence. Such tests, she explains, are not necessarily considered to be accurate or true measures of intelligence, yet they are now being used to make life-and-death decisions. Even if a person has a diminished intellectual capacity, Talbot adds, that does not necessarily mean that he or she lacks a moral sense and cannot distinguish right from wrong. Talbot concludes that using the psychiatric diagnosis of retardation to exclude an entire group of people from capital punishment is questionable. Talbot, a former editor of the* New Republic, *is a senior fellow at the New America Foundation think tank and the author of many articles that have appeared in such publications as the* New York Times Magazine, Salon, *and* Atlantic Monthly.

Most people will never take an I.Q. test, and if they do, it probably won't have a big impact on them. But if you are in the bottom 3 percent of the population that scores 70 or lower, your actual I.Q. number will mean a great deal.

Margaret Talbot, "The Executioner's I.Q. Test," *New York Times Magazine*, June 29, 2003. Copyright © 2003 by The New York Times Company. Reproduced by permission.

Scores in that range will most likely lead to a diagnosis of mental retardation, and that diagnosis will entail many things, starting with mandated special education. Since last June [2002], across the United States, it has also entailed exemption from capital punishment. And so, for someone who has committed a capital crime, an I.Q. score can mean the difference, quite literally, between life and death. It can mean, if we want to be blunt about it, that there is such a thing as being too dumb to die, at least at the hands of the state.

On June 20, 2002, when the Supreme Court issued a decision [*Atkins v. Virginia*] declaring execution of the retarded unconstitutional, it surprised even some of the very people who had been working hardest to make that day come about. . . .

Richard Dieter, executive director of the Death Penalty Information Center in Washington, says that he thought a decision like this was bound to come at some point, but he was still surprised that the court hadn't waited a little longer to see if more state legislatures would ban the practice. Peter Arenella, a U.C.L.A. law professor who says he believes the court was absolutely right in *Atkins*, nonetheless finds the evidence of a public consensus "underwhelming.". . . David Bodiker, the state public defender in Ohio, had waited optimistically for the court's decision in *Atkins*, a Virginia case that centered on a convicted murderer named Daryl Renard Atkins. (Atkins's I.Q. had been tested at 59, but he was sentenced to death nonetheless for the abduction and killing of a young airman from Langley Air Force base.) Bodiker says he knew that the court "would not have taken the case if the justices didn't want to say something new on the subject." But, he says, he is still "somewhat astonished by what they did say, because we never anticipated anything that complete."

Atkins Has Had Surprising Results

In the year since the *Atkins* decision, these are a few of the things it has not done. It has not, as some of its critics predicted, unleashed a flood of farfetched claims. It has not produced flagrant cases of malingering, since in fact it is almost impossible to successfully fake mental retardation, the diagnosis of which involves not only I.Q. scores but documentation of the condition's onset before the age of 18 and assessments of how a person manages day to day, at work, at home and in the community. The person who imagined himself someday staving off execution with a claim of mental retardation would have to have been fiendishly proactive, starting at least in grade school with a purposeful campaign of deflating his test scores and bamboozling his way into special-ed classes. (And would-be fakers who try to flub I.Q. tests as adults don't tend to do it very well; they often make the mistake of answering all the questions wrong, which an actual retarded person rarely does.) It has not led, not yet anyway, to rulings that remove other whole classes of people—like adolescents who commit their crimes at 16 or 17, older than the Supreme Court cutoff for the death penalty but younger than many states permit.[1]

Here is what it has done. It has reopened cases and held out the possibility that a good number of people scheduled to die will spend their lives in prison instead. In Ohio, Bodiker estimates that perhaps 40 of the 207 people on death row may be retarded, and his office has already filed appeals based on the *Atkins* decision for 37 of them. In Virginia, according to Rob Lee, the lawyer who now represents Daryl Atkins, roughly 4 death-row inmates out of the 29 may have claims related to mental retardation. No one has done a national study, but some anti-death-penalty groups estimate that between 5 and 10 percent of the 3,500 people on death row may have mental retardation and therefore be eligible for *Atkins* claims that would save them from execution.

1. In 2004 in *Roper v. Simmons*, the Supreme Court ruled that executing murderers who had committed their crimes before the age of 18 was unconstitutional.

More fundamentally, the *Atkins* decision has heightened or exposed predicaments—about the death penalty, about mental retardation, about the relationship between developmental disabilities and moral agency—that will be with us for a long time to come. For the court majority, and for organizations like the American Association on Mental Retardation, it is clear that mentally retarded people should be exempt from the death penalty because, as a group, they are prone to gullibility and have poor impulse control and limited abstract-reasoning abilities, all of which render them less responsible for their actions—or at least for their death-penalty crimes. Moreover, the same traits, along with a tendency to acquiesce to authority figures, make them more likely to confess to crimes they didn't commit, more likely to waive their rights and less able to participate in their own defense—to remember or provide their lawyer with potentially exonerating details, for example, or to present the jury with a winningly remorseful demeanor. Denis Keyes, a professor of special education at the College of Charleston who serves as an expert witness on cases involving mental retardation, recalls "seeing defendants slouched down in their chairs, scoffing at everything that's said, and that gets a jury mad. Well, there's a good chance the defendant is looking like that because he doesn't have a clue what's going on at the trial."

And yet, to assert that mentally retarded people as a class are less blameworthy for the gravest of crimes is to raise some troubling contradictions. For one thing, a categorical exemption does not chime with the main chords of the disabled-rights movement. In recent years, advocacy for the mentally retarded has been aimed in a very different direction—toward normalization, access, treating individuals as individuals. Some advocates have urged that we drop the label of mental retardation altogether, arguing that it is stigmatizing, arbitrary and bureaucratic. . . .

Intelligence Does Not Equal Morality

In other contexts, it seems obvious that intellectual ability and the capacity to act morally do not always go together. We've all known smart and amoral people, on the one hand, and dense but decent people, on the other. "Whatever conceptualization of moral reasoning you use," says Douglas Mossman, the director of the division of forensic psychiatry at Wright State University in Dayton, Ohio, "you see a range of moral capabilities in people and those capabilities do not necessarily coincide with measures of intelligence or social performance." And as Scalia put it in his dissent, even if there were a connection "between diminished intelligence and the inability to refrain from murder"—a dubious connection to begin with— "what scientific analysis can possibly show that a mildly retarded individual who commits an exquisite torture-killing is 'no more culpable' than the 'average' murderer in a holdup-gone-wrong or a domestic dispute?" Those are moral and legal judgments, after all, not scientific ones.

On the other hand, if the issue is not so much moral agency as it is gullibility and credulity, it is not clear that only people with a diagnosis of retardation are vulnerable. (Plenty of people with no such label are credulous—or there would be no pyramid schemes, Powerball or phone psychics.) And if retarded people are more susceptible to the kind of badgering or leading questioning that produces false confessions, then that's a reason to make interrogations better and fairer (and perhaps a basis for due-process claims).

Use of I.Q. Results Is Problematic

When how a person happens to score on an I.Q. test—a few points below or above 70—can determine life or death, we are surely adding a new element of arbitrariness to a death-penalty system that is already arbitrary in so many other ways. It's not that I.Q. tests are shoddy or unreliable (indeed, they've proved to be remarkably accurate at predicting academic success). But the same person can score differently on them at different times and under different circumstances. The mental retardation label "is useful in that it allows mostly deserving individuals to get services and supports they often desperately need," writes Stephen Greenspan, professor emeritus of educational psychology at the University of Connecticut. "It is fiction in that there is no justification for the idea that there is a magical line (let alone one determinable by a test score) dividing those who have or do not have this condition."

Like other clinical definitions, the American Association on Mental Retardation's definition of the condition has frequently been revised. There have been 10 different versions issued over the last century. And the consequences of these refinements have not been trivial. A lowering of the I.Q. cutoff in 1973, for example, meant that the proportion of the American population classified as mentally retarded plummeted from 16 percent to 3 percent. Such core notions as whether people with mental retardation could ever improve have undergone a great deal of rethinking as well. For years, the standard definitions emphasized the condition's incurability; now they stress its mutability over time, and the power of a good support system to improve or even lift a diagnosis of retardation. Today, some people who might formerly have been classified as retarded are being classified as learning disabled, a different label with different implications. . . .

There Are Different Levels of Mental Retardation

Most retarded people on death row, like most retarded people in general, are in the mildly retarded range—the upper range of the classification, which includes those who can and do, though usually with help, obtain jobs and driver's licenses, take care of themselves, marry, raise children and so on. Retarded people on death row tend not to have Down syndrome, which usually results in more severe retardation. In any case, people with more significant cognitive deficits either lack the capacity to plan or commit a serious crime or are declared incompetent to stand trial. "Drooling guys who don't know how to feed themselves don't end up on the row," as Gregory Meyers, a lawyer in the Ohio public defender's office, puts it.

Many of the people I spoke to for this article pointed out that in making *Atkins* claims, they had to battle against a common misperception of the mentally retarded as more obviously impaired than most mentally retarded people are. They laughed and shook their heads over the stereotypes of slack-jawed guys humming tunelessly to themselves, hulking Lenny types, "Deliverance" extras. "I was at a court proceeding in Florida where there were these two mixed-race defendants who were just gorgeous," Denis Keyes says. "I mean, honey, these two guys took your breath away. And they were retarded, but you could imagine the jury was thinking nobody with mental retardation is that good looking."

But if it's true that many people, even among those who support the death penalty, believe it is wrong to execute the mentally retarded, and at the same time true that many people hold in their minds an inaccurate stereotype of the retarded, then we may have a problem. It may be that the consensus the court identified—holding that it is wrong to execute the mentally retarded but acceptable to execute schizophrenics or minors or people who sustained brain injuries after the age of 18 or people who were unimaginably mistreated—may not be as stable as it seems. . . .

The Logic of the Decision Is Uncertain

Even some of the public defenders eagerly making use of the *Atkins* decision sometimes wonder about the logic of it. "Looking over some of the people on the row, there are people who, O.K., are probably not mentally retarded—maybe they have I.Q.'s of 80," David Bodiker, the Ohio public defender, says. "They have had horrible lives, they flunked out of school, but they don't quite make the grade, so to speak. And you wonder why should there be that distinction? I'm looking down my list of guys on the row, and I see, for instance, David Allen: I.Q. 82. Poor grades. Born premature. Psychiatric problems dating back to age 8. Reginald Brooks. He had an I.Q. of 77 at one time, then 89. Now he's probably got about 91. His problem is more in mental health—schizophrenia."

Bodiker finds it troubling that some inmates perform better on I.Q. tests the longer they've been in prison, which means that while they still suffer from cognitive deficits, they may no longer technically qualify as mentally retarded. Partly they do better because they may be taking an I.Q. test for the fourth or fifth time, reaping the benefits of a practice effect. But more likely, their improved scores reflect the fact that, as Caroline Everington, a forensic mental retardation expert, puts it, "in prison, many of them are living in a stable environment for the first time in their lives." In the strictest sense, these prison-improved scores are unimportant: the focus of the *Atkins* decision is on a person's mental status at the time of the crime, not the time of execution. And I.Q. scores must be backed up with tests of a person's "adaptive functioning." But in a broader way they do matter: they remind you that the elements that make up a diagnosis of mental retardation are fungible. The reasons for that are perfectly legitimate, but when the diagnosis matters in the way it does here, it becomes a little scary. . . .

Blameworthiness—not whether someone did a deed or not, but the extent to which they are culpable for it—is a complicated matter, a matter of whole pictures. It would be a relief, in a way, if a diagnosis like mental retardation always settled the question of how much to blame a guilty person, but it would leave so much out of the picture. And some of those things—moral agency, the nature of the crime itself—might be the very things we care about most.

> "If Atkins does anything in terms of stigma, it de-stigmatizes people with mental disability."

Atkins Will Destigmatize the Mentally Retarded

Christopher Slobogin

While some disability advocates applauded the Atkins v. Virginia *decision, others feared that it could negatively affect the civil rights of the mentally retarded. These critics argued that the decision placed the mentally retarded in a separate class of people who are less culpable for their actions and therefore are essentially incapacitated. This change in their status, opponents contend, could lead to increased stigmatization of the mentally retarded along with an erosion of their civil rights and privileges. In the following selection Christopher Slobogin rebuts these arguments. He contends that rather than placing the mentally retarded in a separate, less competent class of citizens, the decision merely recognizes that the death penalty should be used only against the most depraved murderers in society. Due to their diminished capacity, the mentally retarded can never fall into this category, Slobogin insists. In fact, Slobogin maintains, the decision will destigmatize the mentally retarded because it will correct the common misperception that the mentally retarded are exceptionally dangerous. Slobogin, the author of numerous books and articles, is the Stephen C. O'Connell Professor of Law and the Associate Director of the Center for Children and the Law at the University of Florida Levin College of Law.*

Christopher Slobogin, "Is Atkins the Antithesis or Apotheosis of Antidiscrimination Principles? Sorting Out the Groupwide Effects of Exempting People with Mental Retardation from the Death Penalty," *Alabama Law Review*, Summer 2004. Copyright © 2004 by the *Alabama Law Review*. Reproduced by permission of the publisher and the author.

In *Atkins v. Virginia*, the U.S. Supreme Court held that people with mental retardation may not be executed. Many advocates for people with disability cheered the decision, because it provides a group of disabled people with protection from the harshest punishment imposed by our society. But other disability advocates were dismayed by *Atkins*, not because they are fans of the death penalty, but because they believe that declaring disabled people ineligible for a punishment that is accorded all others denigrates disabled people as something less than human. If people with disability are to be treated equally, these dissenters suggest, they should be treated equally in all areas of the law, including capital sentencing. . . .

My conclusion is that, while *Atkins* is neither the apotheosis nor the antithesis of anti-discrimination principles, overall *Atkins* is good for the disability rights movement and for disabled people. . . .

Some Suggest *Atkins* Will Harm the Mentally Retarded

Probably the best statement of this criticism [of *Atkins* by disability rights activists] comes from Donald Bersoff, a well-known champion of disability rights whose views need to be taken seriously. In a recent *Law & Human Behavior* article, he put forward two complaints about the stigmatizing impact of *Atkins*. First, he wrote, it mischaracterizes the capacities of people with mental retardation. As he put it, "as important as it is to protect those who cannot protect themselves, it is equally important to promote the right of all persons to make their own choices and, as a corollary, to be accountable for those choices." Echoing Justice [Antonin] Scalia [who authored a dissenting opinion in *Atkins*] he then stated, "It is simply untrue that no person with mental retardation is incapable of carrying out a horrible murder with the requisite [degree of] intent or foresight." Secondly, Professor Bersoff suggested that *Atkins* may even lead to a retraction of the rights and privileges that people with disability currently possess. He asserted,

> If we accept the concept of blanket incapacity [which *Atkins* endorses], we relegate people with retardation to second class citizenship, potentially permitting the State to abrogate the exercise of such fundamental interests as the right to marry, to have and rear one's children, to vote, or such everyday entitlements as entering into contracts or making a will.

Mentally Retarded Criminals Are Not Fully Culpable

If true, Professor Bersoff's objections to the *Atkins* majority's "independent evaluation" [of the issue of whether the death penalty is appropriate for the mentally retarded] are potent. I think that his objections are off-base, however. . . . My disagreement with Professor Bersoff can be stated succinctly.

With respect to the mischaracterization issue, it is true, as both Justice Scalia and Professor Bersoff state, that some people with serious mental disability can commit murder with intent and even foresight. I also have doubts about the *Atkins* majority's statement that no mentally retarded person who murders is as culpable or deterrable as the average murderer (and am especially leery of the lesser deterrability assertion, given the evidence that most criminals pay little attention to criminal prohibitions). Nevertheless, I think it is clear that no murderer whose retardation or psychosis contributes to the crime is as culpable as the rare murderer who should be put to death. If we are to have the death penalty, only the most depraved individuals should be executed, as the Court has said over and over again. No person with serious disability is that depraved.

But what about . . . someone like John Penry, who had an IQ in the 60s, but who cased the residence of his victim to make sure she was alone, forced his way in when she grew suspicious of his repairman story, and stabbed her after deciding she might tell the police about the rape? Or someone like [Daryl] Renard Atkins, a mildly retarded individual who, along with another individual, abducted his victim, forced him to withdraw money from an ATM, then took him to a deserted area and shot him eight times? These people intended, and even premeditated their crimes, knowing that they were wrong in doing so.

Only the Most Depraved Can Be Executed

It can be assumed that ... these offenders were legally sane at the time of their crime. Because of their retardation, however, people like ... Penry and Atkins lack the full appreciation of wrongfulness that less disabled people have and that should be required before we can execute someone. While there is not necessarily a directly inverse relationship between intellectual vulnerability and evil, or between madness and badness, the criminal law has long acknowledged that mental and emotional problems compromise the cognitive and volitional capacities that are equated with blameworthiness. As recognized most explicitly by the California Supreme Court in the 1960s, culpability is diminished by an inability to "maturely and meaningfully reflect upon the gravity of the contemplated act." People with retardation, by definition, are compromised in that ability. According to the latest edition of the American Psychiatric Association's Diagnostic and Statistical Manual, even people with "mild" mental retardation at most can develop academic skills up to approximately the sixth-grade level, amounting to the maturity of a twelve year-old. By exempting this whole category of people from its purview, *Atkins* constitutionalized the idea that the death penalty may only be imposed on people who are particularly culpable.

Of course, many people would not draw the line where the *Atkins* majority did. For instance, three separate juries found that Penry was depraved enough to warrant the death penalty. *Atkins*, in essence, held that those juries were wrong in defining depravity so broadly. It also implicitly rejected Justice Scalia's position that the brutality of a murder by itself, regardless of the associated mental state, can make a sane person sufficiently "depraved."

Most importantly for present purposes, *Atkins*'s holding (as distinguished, perhaps, from some of its language about the average murderer) does not mischaracterize the capacities of people with disability in the way Professor Bersoff suggests. *Atkins* does not say that people with retardation are incapable of committing crime with intent or foresight. Nor, of course, does it say that murderers with serious disability should not be held accountable for their choices, as they still can be given life sentences. All *Atkins* says is that people with retardation, even those who commit a "horrible" murder, can never be as evil as the most evil murderers in our society (and thus that the ultimate punishment may not be imposed on them).

Atkins Will De-Stigmatize the Mentally Retarded

For related reasons, I also disagree with Professor Bersoff's claim that *Atkins* will encourage use of categorical disability-based exemptions in the civil rights setting. While people with serious disability never deserve the death penalty, it is an empirical fact, demonstrated by research examining both people with significant mental illness and mental retardation, that even very disabled people can be competent to make treatment decisions and engage in other decision-making tasks. Nothing in *Atkins* can be used to contest that fact, not even its (possibly erroneous) statement that people with retardation cannot be as culpable or deterrable as the average murderer. The inquiry in the civil setting is not whether the disabled person is "average," but whether the person meets a minimum level of competence. In other words, even a person whose capacities are "below average" can, under the law, contract, marry, vote, and so on. Thus, neither the holding nor the unnecessarily broad language of *Atkins* sabotages these types of laws.

If *Atkins* does anything in terms of stigma, it de-stigmatizes people with mental disability. Research clearly shows that, despite the fact that offenders with serious disorders are no more likely to reoffend than the general offender population, the public tends to equate mental disorder with dangerousness. Capital sentencing juries are not immune from this misperception, with the result that they often treat mental disorder not as a mitigating circumstance (as the law requires) but as an aggravating circumstance supporting imposition of the death penalty. *Atkins* can and should be interpreted to mean that this equation of disorder with danger is wrong. Its message should be: we cannot execute people (or do anything else to them) simply because we are irrationally scared of them.

CHAPTER 4

Forbidding the Execution of Juveniles

Chapter Preface

Case Overview: *Donald P. Roper, Superintendent, Potosi Correctional Center v. Christopher Simmons* (2005)

In *Roper v. Simmons* (2005) the U.S. Supreme Court ruled 5-4 that the death penalty is unconstitutional when applied to offenders who were under the age of eighteen at the time they committed their crimes. Citing "changing standards of decency" in the United States, the majority based its opinions on what it described as an "emerging national consensus" that such executions are "cruel and unusual."

Roper involved Christopher Simmons, who as a seventeen-year-old junior at a Missouri high school in September 1993 suggested to two friends that they rob and kill someone. Simmons reportedly reassured his friends that they could get away with committing murder because they were all under the age of eighteen. Although one of the teenagers backed out before the crime, early one morning Simmons and his remaining friend, Charles Benjamin, entered a private house, where Simmons recognized the homeowner, Shirley Crook, as a woman with whom he had previously been in a car accident. Simmons and Benjamin hog-tied Crook with duct tape, drove her to a bridge, and threw her into the water to drown. The culprits made little effort to hide the evidence of the crime: When Shirley Crook's body was discovered the afternoon of the murder, the police were easily able to find Simmons, who was bragging to his friends about the killing. After being arrested the following day, Simmons confessed to the crime; he was ultimately found guilty of murder. During the sentencing phase of the trial the prosecution easily proved three aggravating factors, and the jury sentenced Simmons to death in spite of both character testimony from Simmons's family and friends and the defense attorney's attempts to argue that seventeen-year-olds should not be considered mature enough to take full responsibility for their crimes. On appeal, the Missouri Supreme Court ruled on August 26, 2003, that juvenile executions violated the Eighth Amendment and vacated Simmons's death sentence. The prosecution appealed, and the U.S. Supreme Court agreed to hear the case.

The question of juvenile capital punishment had been visited by the Court before. In previous cases, most recently *Stanford v. Kentucky* (1989), the justices had ruled that while the death penalty should not be applied to those who were under the age of sixteen when they committed their crimes, those sixteen and older should be dealt with as if they are mature adults. In *Roper*, writing for the majority, Justice Anthony Kennedy concluded that the execution of juveniles was opposed by a national consensus that had emerged in the United States since the *Stanford* decision. Kennedy also stated that the existence of this national consensus was confirmed by the fact that "the United States stands alone" in the world as a country that allows the execution of juveniles. Writing in dissent, Justices Antonin Scalia, William Rehnquist, and Clarence Thomas argued angrily that the Supreme Court should not consider international opinion when deciding the constitutionality of American laws. In a separate dissent Justice Sandra Day O'Connor argued that while international opinion should be considered, the majority had erred in identifying a clear "national consensus," which in her opinion did not exist. Regardless, as of March 2005 those in the United States who commit crimes while under the age of eighteen are no longer eligible for the death penalty.

> *"The differences between juvenile and adult offenders are too marked and well understood to risk allowing a youthful person to receive the death penalty despite insufficient culpability."*

The Court's Opinion: Executing Juveniles Is Unconstitutional

Anthony M. Kennedy

In the Supreme Court's opinion in Roper v. Simmons, *excerpted here, Justice Anthony M. Kennedy outlined the majority's rationale for the decision that the execution of those who were under eighteen when they committed their crimes is unconstitutional. Kennedy contended that juveniles are less mature and more susceptible to peer pressure than are adults and that they lack a fully developed character. For these reasons, he concluded, juveniles should not be held to the same standards of culpability as should adults and should not be eligible for the death penalty. In one of the most contentious points of the opinion, Kennedy pointed out that the United States "stands alone" as a nation that endorses the death penalty for juveniles. While he acknowledged that international law does not bear on Supreme Court decisions, he argued that the world's condemnation of juvenile executions provided "significant confirmation" for the Court. Kennedy was nominated to the U.S. Supreme Court by President Ronald Reagan and took his oath of office in February 1988.*

Anthony M. Kennedy, majority opinion, *Donald P. Roper, Superintendent, Potosi Correctional Center v. Christopher Simmons*, U.S. Supreme Court, March 1, 2005.

This case requires us to address, for the second time in a decade and a half, whether it is permissible under the Eighth and Fourteenth Amendments to the Constitution of the United States to execute a juvenile offender who was older than 15 but younger than 18 when he committed a capital crime. In *Stanford v. Kentucky* (1989), a divided Court rejected the proposition that the Constitution bars capital punishment for juvenile offenders in this age group. We reconsider the question. . . .

The Death Penalty Needs Special Consideration

A majority of States have rejected the imposition of the death penalty on juvenile offenders under 18, and we now hold this is required by the Eighth Amendment.

Because the death penalty is the most severe punishment, the Eighth Amendment applies to it with special force. Capital punishment must be limited to those offenders who commit "a narrow category of the most serious crimes" and whose extreme culpability makes them "the most deserving of execution." *Atkins* [*v. Virginia* (2002)]. This principle is implemented throughout the capital sentencing process. States must give narrow and precise definition to the aggravating factors that can result in a capital sentence. In any capital case a defendant has wide latitude to raise as a mitigating factor "any aspect of [his or her] character or record and any of the circumstances of the offense that the defendant proffers as a basis for a sentence less than death." *Lockett v. Ohio* (1978) (plurality opinion). There are a number of crimes that beyond question are severe in absolute terms, yet the death penalty may not be imposed for their commission. The death penalty may not be imposed on certain classes of offenders, such as juveniles under 16, the insane, and the mentally retarded, no matter how heinous the crime. These rules vindicate the underlying principle that the death penalty is reserved for a narrow category of crimes and offenders.

Juveniles Are Qualitatively Different than Adults

Three general differences between juveniles under 18 and adults demonstrate that juvenile offenders cannot with reliability be classified among the worst offenders. First, as any parent knows and as the scientific and sociological studies respondent and his *amici* cite tend to confirm, "[a] lack of maturity and an underdeveloped sense of responsibility are found in youth more often than in adults and are more understandable among the young. These qualities often result in impetuous and ill-considered actions and decisions." *Johnson* [*v. Texas* (1993)]. It has been noted [by J. Arnett] that "adolescents are overrepresented statistically in virtually every category of reckless behavior." In recognition of the comparative immaturity and irresponsibility of juveniles, almost every State prohibits those under 18 years of age from voting, serving on juries, or marrying without parental consent.

The second area of difference is that juveniles are more vulnerable or susceptible to negative influences and outside pressures, including peer pressure. This is explained in part by the prevailing circumstance that juveniles have less control, or less experience with control, over their own environment.

The third broad difference is that the character of a juvenile is not as well formed as that of an adult. The personality traits of juveniles are more transitory, less fixed.

Juveniles Have Diminished Culpability

These differences render suspect any conclusion that a juvenile falls among the worst offenders. The susceptibility of juveniles to immature and irresponsible behavior means "their irresponsible conduct is not as morally reprehensible as that of an adult." *Thompson* [*v. Oklahoma* (1988)] (plurality opinion).

Their own vulnerability and comparative lack of control over their immediate surroundings mean juveniles have a greater claim than adults to be forgiven for failing to escape negative influences in their whole environment. The reality that juveniles still struggle to define their identity means it is less supportable to conclude that even a heinous crime committed by a juvenile is evidence of irretrievably depraved character. From a moral standpoint it would be misguided to equate the failings of a minor with those of an adult, for a greater possibility exists that a minor's character deficiencies will be reformed. Indeed, "[t]he relevance of youth as a mitigating factor derives from the fact that the signature qualities of youth are transient; as individuals mature, the impetuousness and recklessness that may dominate in younger years can subside." *Johnson*.

In *Thompson*, a plurality of the Court recognized the import of these characteristics with respect to juveniles under 16, and relied on them to hold that the Eighth Amendment prohibited the imposition of the death penalty on juveniles below that age. We conclude the same reasoning applies to all juvenile offenders under 18.

Once the diminished culpability of juveniles is recognized, it is evident that the penological justifications for the death penalty apply to them with lesser force than to adults. We have held there are two distinct social purposes served by the death penalty: "'retribution and deterrence of capital crimes by prospective offenders.'" *Atkins* (quoting *Gregg v. Georgia* (1976) (joint opinion of Stewart, Powell, and Stevens, JJ.)). As for retribution, we remarked in *Atkins* that "[i]f the culpability of the average murderer is insufficient to justify the most extreme sanction available to the State, the lesser culpability of the mentally retarded offender surely does not merit that form of retribution." The same conclusions follow from the lesser culpability of the juvenile offender. Whether viewed as an attempt to express the community's moral outrage or as an attempt to right the balance for the wrong to the victim, the case for retribution is not as strong with a minor as with an adult. Retribution is not proportional if the law's most severe penalty is imposed on one whose culpability or blameworthiness is diminished, to a substantial degree, by reason of youth and immaturity.

As for deterrence, it is unclear whether the death penalty has a significant or even measurable deterrent effect on juveniles, as counsel for the petitioner acknowledged at oral argument. In general we leave to legislatures the assessment of the efficacy of various criminal penalty schemes. Here, however, the absence of evidence of deterrent effect is of special concern because the same characteristics that render juveniles less culpable than adults suggest as well that juveniles will be less susceptible to deterrence. In particular, as the plurality observed in *Thompson*, "[t]he likelihood that the teenage offender has made the kind of cost-benefit analysis that attaches any weight to the possibility of execution is so remote as to be virtually nonexistent." To the extent the juvenile death penalty might have residual deterrent effect, it is worth noting that the punishment of life imprisonment without the possibility of parole is itself a severe sanction, in particular for a young person.

Exceptional Juvenile Defendants Are Irrelevant

In concluding that neither retribution nor deterrence provides adequate justification for imposing the death penalty on juvenile offenders, we cannot deny or overlook the brutal crimes too many juvenile offenders have committed. Certainly it can be argued, although we by no means concede the point, that a rare case might arise in which a juvenile offender has sufficient psychological maturity, and at the same time demonstrates sufficient depravity, to merit a sentence of death. Indeed, this possibility is the linchpin of one contention pressed by petitioner and his *amici*. They assert that even assuming the truth of the observations we have made about juveniles' diminished culpability in general, jurors nonetheless should be allowed to consider mitigating arguments related to youth on a case-by-case basis, and in some cases to impose the death penalty if justified. A central feature of death penalty sentencing is a particular assessment of the circumstances of the crime and the characteristics of the offender. The system is designed to consider both aggravating and mitigating circumstances, including youth, in every case. Given this Court's own insistence on individualized consideration, petitioner maintains that it is both arbitrary and unnecessary to adopt a categorical rule barring imposition of the death penalty on any offender under 18 years of age.

We disagree. The differences between juvenile and adult offenders are too marked and well understood to risk allowing a youthful person to receive the death penalty despite insufficient culpability. An unacceptable likelihood exists that the brutality or cold-blooded nature of any particular crime would overpower mitigating arguments based on youth as a matter of course, even where the juvenile offender's objective immaturity, vulnerability, and lack of true depravity should require a sentence less severe than death. In some cases a defendant's youth may even be counted against him. In this very case, as we noted above, the prosecutor argued [Christopher] Simmons' youth was aggravating rather than mitigating. While this sort of overreaching could be corrected by a particular rule to ensure that the mitigating force of youth is not overlooked, that would not address our larger concerns.

It is difficult even for expert psychologists to differentiate between the juvenile offender whose crime reflects unfortunate yet transient immaturity, and the rare juvenile offender whose crime reflects irreparable corruption. As we understand it, this difficulty underlies the rule forbidding psychiatrists from diagnosing any patient under 18 as having antisocial personality disorder, a disorder also referred to as psychopathy or sociopathy, and which is characterized by callousness, cynicism, and contempt for the feelings, rights, and suffering of others. If trained psychiatrists with the advantage of clinical testing and observation refrain, despite diagnostic expertise, from assessing any juvenile under 18 as having antisocial personality disorder, we conclude that States should refrain from asking jurors to issue a far graver condemnation—that a juvenile offender merits the death penalty. When a juvenile offender commits a heinous crime, the State can exact forfeiture of some of the most basic liberties, but the State cannot extinguish his life and his potential to attain a mature understanding of his own humanity.

18 Is a Good Age to Draw the Line

Drawing the line at 18 years of age is subject, of course, to the objections always raised against categorical rules. The qualities that distinguish juveniles from adults do not disappear when an individual turns 18. By the same token, some under 18 have already attained a level of maturity some adults will never reach. For the reasons we have discussed, however, a line must be drawn. The plurality opinion in *Thompson* drew the line at 16. In the intervening years the *Thompson* plurality's conclusion that offenders under 16 may not be executed has not been challenged. The logic of *Thompson* extends to those who are under 18. The age of 18 is the point where society draws the line for many purposes between childhood and adulthood. It is, we conclude, the age at which the line for death eligibility ought to rest. . . .

No Other Countries Allow Juvenile Executions

Our determination that the death penalty is disproportionate punishment for offenders under 18 finds confirmation in the stark reality that the United States is the only country in the world that continues to give official sanction to the juvenile death penalty. This reality does not become controlling, for the task of interpreting the Eighth Amendment remains our responsibility. Yet at least from the time of the Court's decision in *Trop* [*v. Dulles* (1958)], the Court has referred to the laws of other countries and to international authorities as instructive for its interpretation of the Eighth Amendment's prohibition of "cruel and unusual punishments." ("The civilized nations of the world are in virtual unanimity that statelessness is not to be imposed as punishment for crime"); see also *Atkins* (recognizing that "within the world community, the imposition of the death penalty for crimes committed by mentally retarded offenders is overwhelmingly disapproved"); *Thompson* (plurality opinion) (noting the abolition of the juvenile death penalty "by other nations that share our Anglo-American heritage, and by the leading members of the Western European community," and observing that "[w]e have previously recognized the relevance of the views of the international community in determining whether a punishment is cruel and unusual"); *Enmund* [*v. Florida* (1982)] (observing that "the doctrine of felony murder has been abolished in England and India, severely restricted in Canada and a number of other Commonwealth countries, and is unknown in continental Europe"); *Coker* [*v. Georgia* (1977)] (plurality opinion) ("It is ... not irrelevant here that out of 60 major nations in the world surveyed in 1965, only 3 retained the death penalty for rape where death did not ensue").

As respondent and a number of *amici* emphasize, Article 37 of the United Nations Convention on the Rights of the Child, which every country in the world has ratified save for the United States and Somalia, contains an express prohibition on capital punishment for crimes committed by juveniles under 18. No ratifying country has entered a reservation to the provision prohibiting the execution of juvenile offenders. Parallel prohibitions are contained in other significant international covenants.

Respondent and his *amici* have submitted, and petitioner does not contest, that only seven countries other than the United States have executed juvenile offenders since 1990: Iran, Pakistan, Saudi Arabia, Yemen, Nigeria, the Democratic Republic of Congo, and China. Since then each of these countries has either abolished capital punishment for juveniles or made public disavowal of the practice. In sum, it is fair to say that the United States now stands alone in a world that has turned its face against the juvenile death penalty. . . .

It is proper that we acknowledge the overwhelming weight of international opinion against the juvenile death penalty, resting in large part on the understanding that the instability and emotional imbalance of young people may often be a factor in the crime. The opinion of the world community, while not controlling our outcome, does provide respected and significant confirmation for our own conclusions. . . .

It does not lessen our fidelity to the Constitution or our pride in its origins to acknowledge that the express affirmation of certain fundamental rights by other nations and peoples simply underscores the centrality of those same rights within our own heritage of freedom.

The Eighth and Fourteenth Amendments forbid imposition of the death penalty on offenders who were under the age of 18 when their crimes were committed. The judgment of the Missouri Supreme Court setting aside the sentence of death imposed upon Christopher Simmons is affirmed.

> "The fact that juveniles are generally less culpable for their misconduct than adults does not necessarily mean that a 17-year-old murderer cannot be sufficiently culpable to merit the death penalty."

Dissenting Opinion: There Is No National Consensus Against Executing Juveniles

Sandra Day O'Connor

In the following excerpt from her dissenting opinion in Roper v. Simmons, *Justice Sandra Day O'Connor argued that the execution of juveniles is not forbidden by the Eighth Amendment prohibition against cruel and unusual punishment because there does not yet exist a clear national consensus that such executions are improper. In addition, O'Connor contended that the majority of the Court had failed to offer evidence to support the claim that those under eighteen cannot be culpable of murder. She argued that there was no basis for the majority's decision to establish eighteen as the age at which a murderer becomes eligible for execution and concluded that the juvenile death penalty does not represent an unconstitutional punishment. O'Connor was appointed to the Supreme Court in 1981 by President Ronald Reagan, thus becoming the first woman Supreme Court justice in U.S. history; she announced her retirement from the Court in June 2005.*

Sandra Day O'Connor, dissenting opinion, *Donald P. Roper, Superintendent, Potosi Correctional Center v. Christopher Simmons*, U.S. Supreme Court, March 1, 2005.

The Court's decision today establishes a categorical rule forbidding the execution of any offender for any crime committed before his 18th birthday, no matter how deliberate, wanton, or cruel the offense. Neither the objective evidence of contemporary societal values, nor the Court's moral proportionality analysis, nor the two in tandem suffice to justify this ruling.

Although the Court finds support for its decision in the fact that a majority of the States now disallow capital punishment of 17-year-old offenders, it refrains from asserting that its holding is compelled by a genuine national consensus. Indeed, the evidence before us fails to demonstrate conclusively that any such consensus has emerged in the brief period since we upheld the constitutionality of this practice in *Stanford v. Kentucky* (1989).

Insufficient Evidence

Instead, the rule decreed by the Court rests, ultimately, on its independent moral judgment that death is a disproportionately severe punishment for any 17-year-old offender. I do not subscribe to this judgment. Adolescents *as a class* are undoubtedly less mature, and therefore less culpable for their misconduct, than adults. But the Court has adduced no evidence impeaching the seemingly reasonable conclusion reached by many state legislatures: that at least *some* 17-year-old murderers are sufficiently mature to deserve the death penalty in an appropriate case. Nor has it been shown that capital sentencing juries are incapable of accurately assessing a youthful defendant's maturity or of giving due weight to the mitigating characteristics associated with youth.

On this record—and especially in light of the fact that so little has changed since our recent decision in *Stanford*—I would not substitute our judgment about the moral propriety of capital punishment for 17-year-old murderers for the judgments of the Nation's legislatures. Rather, I would demand a clearer showing that our society truly has set its face against this practice before reading the Eighth Amendment categorically to forbid it. . . .

The Legislatures Disagree

In determining whether the juvenile death penalty comports with contemporary standards of decency, our inquiry begins with the "clearest and most reliable objective evidence of contemporary values"—the actions of the Nation's legislatures. [*Penry v. Lynaugh* (1989)]. As the Court emphasizes, the overall number of jurisdictions that currently disallow the execution of under-18 offenders is the same as the number that forbade the execution of mentally retarded offenders when *Atkins* [*v. Virginia* (2002)] was decided. At present, 12 States and the District of Columbia do not have the death penalty, while an additional 18 States and the Federal Government authorize capital punishment but prohibit the execution of under-18 offenders. And here, as in *Atkins*, only a very small fraction of the States that permit capital punishment of offenders within the relevant class has actually carried out such an execution in recent history: Six States have executed under-18 offenders in the 16 years since *Stanford*, while five States had executed mentally retarded offenders in the 13 years prior to *Atkins*. In these respects, the objective evidence in this case is, indeed, "similar, and in some respects parallel to" the evidence upon which we relied in *Atkins*.

While the similarities between the two cases are undeniable, the objective evidence of national consensus is marginally weaker here. Most importantly, in *Atkins* there was significant evidence of *opposition* to the execution of the mentally retarded, but there was virtually no countervailing evidence of affirmative legislative *support* for this practice. The States that permitted such executions did so only because they had not enacted any prohibitory legislation. Here, by contrast, at least eight States have current statutes that specifically set 16 or 17 as the minimum age at which commission of a capital crime can expose the offender to the death penalty. Five of these eight States presently have one or more juvenile offenders on death row (six if respondent is included in the count), and four of them have executed at least one under-18 offender in the past 15 years. In all, there are currently over 70 juvenile offenders on death row in 12 different States (13 including respondent). This evidence suggests some measure of continuing public support for the availability of the death penalty for 17-year-old capital murderers.

Moreover, the Court in *Atkins* made clear that it was "not so much the number of [States forbidding execution of the mentally retarded] that [was] significant, but the consistency of the direction of change." In contrast to the trend in *Atkins*, the States have not moved uniformly towards abolishing the juvenile death penalty. Instead, since our decision in *Stanford*, two States have expressly reaffirmed their support for this practice by enacting statutes setting 16 as the minimum age for capital punishment. Furthermore, as the Court emphasized in *Atkins* itself, at the pace of legislative action in this context has been considerably slower than it was with regard to capital punishment of the mentally retarded. In the 13 years between our decisions in *Penry* and *Atkins*, no fewer than 16 States banned the execution of mentally retarded offenders. By comparison, since our decision 16 years ago in *Stanford*, only four States that previously permitted the execution of under-18 offenders, plus the Federal Government, have legislatively reversed course, and one additional State's high court has construed the State's death penalty statute not to apply to under-18 offenders. The slower pace of change is no doubt partially attributable, as the Court says, to the fact that 11 States had already imposed a minimum age of 18 when *Stanford* was decided. Nevertheless, the extraordinary wave of legislative action leading up to our decision in *Atkins* provided strong evidence that the country truly had set itself against capital punishment of the mentally retarded. Here, by contrast, the halting pace of change gives reason for pause.

Evidence of National Consensus Is Weak

To the extent that the objective evidence supporting today's decision is similar to that in *Atkins*, this merely highlights the fact that such evidence is not dispositive in either of the two cases. After all, as the Court today confirms, the Constitution requires that "'in the end our own judgment ... be brought to bear'" in deciding whether the Eighth Amendment forbids a particular punishment. This judgment is not merely a rubber stamp on the tally of legislative and jury actions. Rather, it is an integral part of the Eighth Amendment inquiry—and one that is entitled to independent weight in reaching our ultimate decision.

Here, as in *Atkins*, the objective evidence of a national consensus is weaker than in most prior cases in which the Court has struck down a particular punishment under the Eighth Amendment. In my view, the objective evidence of national consensus, standing alone, was insufficient to dictate the Court's holding in *Atkins*. Rather, the compelling moral proportionality argument against capital punishment of mentally retarded offenders played a *decisive* role in persuading the Court that the practice was inconsistent with the Eighth Amendment. Indeed, the force of the proportionality argument in *Atkins* significantly bolstered the Court's confidence that the objective evidence in that case did, in fact, herald the emergence of a genuine national consensus. Here, by contrast, the proportionality argument against the juvenile death penalty is so flawed that it can be given little, if any, analytical weight—it proves too weak to resolve the lingering ambiguities in the objective evidence of legislative consensus or to justify the Court's categorical rule.

Juveniles Can Be Fully Culpable

Seventeen-year-old murderers must be categorically exempted from capital punishment, the Court says, because they "cannot with reliability be classified among the worst offenders." That conclusion is premised on three perceived differences between "adults," who have already reached their 18th birthdays, and "juveniles," who have not. First, juveniles lack maturity and responsibility and are more reckless than adults. Second, juveniles are more vulnerable to outside influences because they have less control over their surroundings. And third, a juvenile's character is not as fully formed as that of an adult. Based on these characteristics, the Court determines that 17-year-old capital murderers are not as blameworthy as adults guilty of similar crimes; that 17-year-olds are less likely than adults to be deterred by the prospect of a death sentence; and that it is difficult to conclude that a 17-year-old who commits even the most heinous of crimes is "irretrievably depraved." The Court suggests that "a rare case might arise in which a juvenile offender has sufficient psychological maturity, and at the same time demonstrates sufficient depravity, to merit a sentence of death." However, the Court argues that a categorical age-based prohibition is justified as a prophylactic rule because "[t]he differences between juvenile and adult offenders are too marked and well understood to risk allowing a youthful person to receive the death penalty despite insufficient culpability."

It is beyond cavil that juveniles as a class are generally less mature, less responsible, and less fully formed than adults, and that these differences bear on juveniles' comparative moral culpability. See, *e.g., Johnson v. Texas* (1993) ("There is no dispute that a defendant's youth is a relevant mitigating circumstance"); (O'Connor, J., dissenting) ("[T]he vicissitudes of youth bear directly on the young offender's culpability and responsibility for the crime"); *Eddings* [*v. Oklahoma* (1982)], ("Our history is replete with laws and judicial recognition that minors, especially in their earlier years, generally are less mature and responsible than adults"). But even accepting this premise, the Court's proportionality argument fails to support its categorical rule.

First, the Court adduces no evidence whatsoever in support of its sweeping conclusion that it is only in "rare" cases, if ever, that 17-year-old murderers are sufficiently mature and act with sufficient depravity to warrant the death penalty. The fact that juveniles are generally *less* culpable for their misconduct than adults does not necessarily mean that a 17-year-old murderer cannot be *sufficiently* culpable to merit the death penalty. At most, the Court's argument suggests that the average 17-year-old murderer is not as culpable as the average adult murderer. But an especially depraved juvenile offender may nevertheless be just as culpable as many adult offenders considered bad enough to deserve the death penalty. Similarly, the fact that the availability of the death penalty may be *less* likely to deter a juvenile from committing a capital crime does not imply that this threat cannot *effectively* deter some 17-year-olds from such an act. Surely there is an age below which no offender, no matter what his crime, can be deemed to have the cognitive or emotional maturity necessary to warrant the death penalty. But at least at the margins between adolescence and adulthood—and especially for 17-year-olds such as respondent—the relevant differences between "adults" and "juveniles" appear to be a matter of degree, rather than of kind. It follows that a legislature may reasonably conclude that at least *some* 17-year-olds can act with sufficient moral culpability, and can be sufficiently deterred by the threat of execution, that capital punishment may be warranted in an appropriate case. . . .

There Is No Clear Dividing Line

The Court's proportionality argument suffers from a second and closely related defect: It fails to establish that the differences in maturity between 17-year-olds and young "adults" are both universal enough and significant enough to justify a bright-line prophylactic rule against capital punishment of the former. The Court's analysis is premised on differences *in the aggregate* between juveniles and adults, which frequently do not hold true when comparing individuals. Although it may be that many 17-year-old murderers lack sufficient maturity to deserve the death penalty, some juvenile murderers may be quite mature. Chronological age is not an unfailing measure of psychological development, and common experience suggests that many 17-year-olds are more mature than the average young "adult." In short, the class of offenders exempted from capital punishment by today's decision is too broad and too diverse to warrant a categorical prohibition. Indeed, the age-based line drawn by the Court is indefensibly arbitrary—it quite likely will protect a number of offenders who are mature enough to deserve the death penalty and may well leave vulnerable many who are not. . . .

The Role of International Opinion

I turn, finally, to the Court's discussion of foreign and international law. Without question, there has been a global trend in recent years towards abolishing capital punishment for under-18 offenders. Very few, if any, countries other than the United States now permit this practice in law or in fact. While acknowledging that the actions and views of other countries do not dictate the outcome of our Eighth Amendment inquiry, the Court asserts that "the overwhelming weight of international opinion against the juvenile death penalty . . . does provide respected and significant confirmation for [its] own conclusions." Because I do not believe that a genuine *national* consensus against the juvenile death penalty has yet developed, and because I do not believe the Court's moral proportionality argument justifies a categorical, age-based constitutional rule, I can assign no such *confirmatory* role to the international consensus described by the Court. In short, the evidence of an international consensus does not alter my determination that the Eighth Amendment does not, at this time, forbid capital punishment of 17-year-old murderers in all cases.

Nevertheless, I disagree with Justice [Antonin] Scalia's contention that foreign and international law have no place in our Eighth Amendment jurisprudence. Over the course of nearly half a century, the Court has consistently referred to foreign and international law as relevant to its assessment of evolving standards of decency. This inquiry reflects the special character of the Eighth Amendment, which, as the Court has long held, draws its meaning directly from the maturing values of civilized society. Obviously, American law is distinctive in many respects, not least where the specific provisions of our Constitution and the history of its exposition so dictate. But this Nation's evolving understanding of human dignity certainly is neither wholly isolated from, nor inherently at odds with, the values prevailing in other countries. On the contrary, we should not be surprised to find congruence between domestic and international values, especially where the international community has reached clear agreement—expressed in international law or in the domestic laws of individual countries—that a particular form of punishment is inconsistent with fundamental human rights. At least, the existence of an international consensus of this nature can serve to confirm the reasonableness of a consonant and genuine American consensus. The instant case presents no such domestic consensus, however, and the recent emergence of an otherwise global consensus does not alter that basic fact....

Reasonable minds can differ as to the minimum age at which commission of a serious crime should expose the defendant to the death penalty, if at all. Many jurisdictions have abolished capital punishment altogether, while many others have determined that even the most heinous crime, if committed before the age of 18, should not be punishable by death. Indeed, were my office that of a legislator, rather than a judge, then I, too, would be inclined to support legislation setting a minimum age of 18 in this context. But a significant number of States, including Missouri, have decided to make the death penalty potentially available for 17-year-old capital murderers such as respondent. Without a clearer showing that a genuine national consensus forbids the execution of such offenders, this Court should not substitute its own "inevitably subjective judgment" on how best to resolve this difficult moral question for the judgments of the Nation's democratically elected legislatures. I respectfully dissent.

> "This fresh understanding of adolescence does not excuse juvenile offenders from punishment for violent crime, but it clearly lessens their culpability."

Juveniles Are Less Culpable than Adults

American Bar Association

In the following selection, published prior to the Supreme Court's ruling in Roper v. Simmons, *the American Bar Association (ABA) cited the latest scientific evidence to demonstrate that juveniles and adults should be treated differently by society. Pointing to evidence that juvenile brains are physically still changing and developing through adolescence, the ABA argued that juveniles are not yet adults in mental, physical, or emotional terms. These physical realities, the ABA concluded, do not excuse juveniles from punishment for crimes, but they do lessen the culpability of juvenile offenders. Given the Court's decision in* Atkins v. Virginia *that execution of the mentally retarded is unconstitutional because the mentally retarded are less culpable for crimes, the ABA argued that the Court should also strike down execution of the young. This sort of scientific evidence proved important to the case because it affected the justices' thinking about the difference between juveniles and adults. The American Bar Association, which was founded in 1878, has over four hundred thousand members and is the most important national organization of the legal profession in the United States.*

American Bar Association, "Cruel and Unusual Punishment: The Juvenile Death Penalty: Adolescence, Brain Development, and Legal Culpability," www.abanet.org, January 2004. Copyright © 2004 by the National Juvenile Defender Center. Reproduced by permission.

The Death Penalty

In 2002, the U.S. Supreme Court banned the execution of mentally retarded persons. This decision, *Atkins v. Virginia*, cited the underdeveloped mental capacities of those with mental retardation as a major factor behind the Justices' decision.

Adolescence is a transitional period during which a child is becoming, but is not yet, an adult. An adolescent is at a crossroads of changes where emotions, hormones, judgment, identity and the physical body are so in flux that parents and even experts struggle to fully understand.

As a society, we recognize the limitations of adolescents and, therefore, restrict their privileges to vote, serve on a jury, consume alcohol, marry, enter into contracts, and even watch movies with mature content. Each year, the United States spends billions of dollars to promote drug use prevention and sex education to protect youth at this vulnerable stage of life. When it comes to the death penalty, however, we treat them as fully functioning adults.

The Basics of the Human Brain

The human brain has been called the most complex three-pound mass in the known universe. This is a well deserved reputation, for this organ contains billions of connections among its parts and governs countless actions, involuntary and voluntary, physical, mental and emotional.

The largest part of the brain is the *frontal lobe*. A small area of the frontal lobe located behind the forehead, called the *pre-frontal cortex*, controls the brain's most advanced functions. This part, often referred to as the "CEO" of the body, provides humans with advanced cognition. It allows us to prioritize thoughts, imagine, think in the abstract, anticipate consequences, plan, and control impulses.

Along with everything else in the body, the brain changes significantly during adolescence. In the last five years, scientists, using new technologies, have discovered that adolescent brains are far less developed than previously believed.

New Technology, New Discoveries

Scientists are now utilizing advances in magnetic resonance imaging (MRI) to create and study three-dimensional images of the brain without the use of radiation (as in an x-ray). This breakthrough allows scientists to safely scan children over many years, tracking the development of their brains.

Researchers at Harvard Medical School, the National Institute of Mental Health, UCLA, and others, are collaborating to "map" the development of the brain from childhood to adulthood and examine its implications.

The scientists, to their surprise, discovered that the teenage brain undergoes an intense overproduction of *gray matter* (the brain tissue that does the "thinking"). Then a period of "pruning" takes over, during which the brain discards gray matter at a rapid rate. This process is similar to pruning a tree: cutting back branches stimulates health and growth.

In the brain, pruning is accompanied by *myelination*, a process in which *white matter* develops. White matter is fatty tissue that serves as insulation for the brain's circuitry, making the brain's operation more precise and efficient.

Researchers have carefully scrutinized the pace and severity of these changes and have learned that they continue into a person's early 20s. Dr. Elizabeth Sowell, a member of the UCLA brain research team, has led studies of brain development from adolescence to adulthood. She and her colleagues found that the frontal lobe undergoes far more change during adolescence than at any other stage of life. It is also the last part of the brain to develop, which means that even as they become fully capable in other areas, adolescents cannot reason as well as adults: "[m]aturation, particularly in the frontal lobes, has been shown to correlate with measures of cognitive functioning."

Biology and Behavior

Jay Giedd, a researcher at the National Institute of Mental Health, explains that during adolescence the "part of the brain that is helping organization, planning and strategizing is not done being built yet. . . . It's sort of unfair to expect [adolescents] to have adult levels of organizational skills or decision making before their brain is finished being built."

Dr. Deborah Yurgelun-Todd of Harvard Medical School has studied the relation between these new findings and teen behavior and concluded that adolescents often rely on emotional parts of the brain, rather than the frontal lobe. She explains, "one of the things that teenagers seem to do is to respond more strongly with gut response than they do with evaluating the consequences of what they're doing."

Also, appearances may be deceiving: "Just because they're physically mature, they may not appreciate the consequences or weigh information the same way as adults do. So we may be mistaken if we think that [although] somebody looks physically mature, their brain may in fact not be mature."

This discovery gives us a new understanding into juvenile delinquency. The frontal lobe is "involved in behavioral facets germane to many aspects of criminal culpability," explains Dr. Ruben C. Gur, neuropsychologist and Director of the Brain Behavior Laboratory at the University of Pennsylvania. "Perhaps most relevant is the involvement of these brain regions in the control of aggression and other impulses. . . . If the neural substrates of these behaviors have not reached maturity before adulthood, it is unreasonable to expect the behaviors themselves to reflect mature thought processes.

Forbidding the Execution of Juveniles

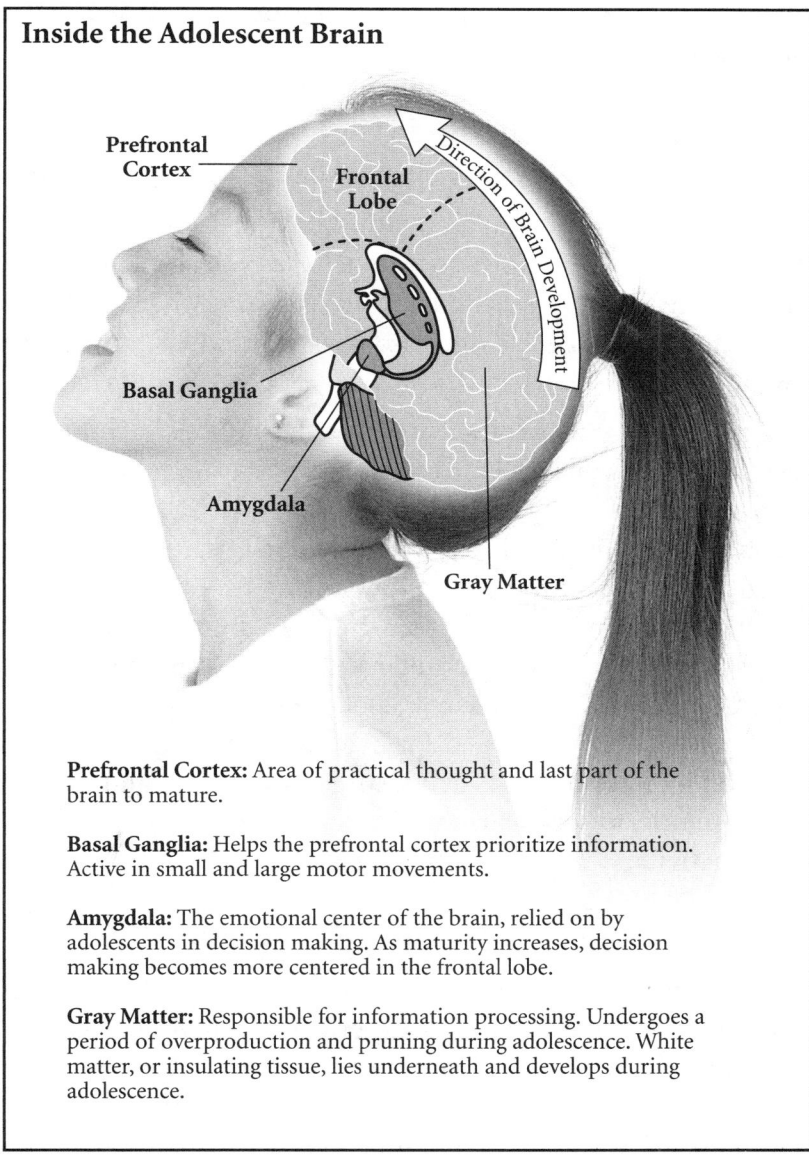

Inside the Adolescent Brain

Prefrontal Cortex: Area of practical thought and last part of the brain to mature.

Basal Ganglia: Helps the prefrontal cortex prioritize information. Active in small and large motor movements.

Amygdala: The emotional center of the brain, relied on by adolescents in decision making. As maturity increases, decision making becomes more centered in the frontal lobe.

Gray Matter: Responsible for information processing. Undergoes a period of overproduction and pruning during adolescence. White matter, or insulating tissue, lies underneath and develops during adolescence.

"The evidence now is strong that the brain does not cease to mature until the early 20s in those relevant parts that govern impulsivity, judgment, planning for the future, foresight of consequences, and other characteristics that make people morally culpable.... Indeed, age 21 or 22 would be closer to the 'biological' age of maturity."

Other Changes in the Body

In addition to the profound physical changes of the brain, adolescents also undergo dramatic hormonal and emotional changes. One of the hormones which has the most dramatic effect on the body is testosterone. Testosterone, which is closely associated with aggression, increases tenfold in adolescent boys.

Emotionally, an adolescent "is really both part child and part adult," explains Melvin Lewis, an expert in child psychiatry and pediatrics at Yale University School of Medicine. Normal development at this time includes self-searching, during which the adolescent tries to grow out of his or her childlike self. This change is complicated by the conflict between an adolescent's new sense of adult identity and remaining juvenile insecurities. The behaviors associated with this process include self-absorption, a need for privacy, mood swings, unique dress, and escapism, such as video games, music, and talking on the phone, as well as riskier behaviors, such as drug use or sexual activity.

Childhood Abuse and Violence

In addition to this context of change and volatility, research shows that abusive childhood experiences can trigger violent behavior. The American Academy of Pediatrics has identified several risk factors that can spark violence in adolescents, including being witness to domestic violence or substance abuse within the family, being poorly or inappropriately supervised, and being the victim of physical or sexual assault.

Researcher Phyllis L. Crocker of Cleveland-Marshall College of Law has written that "the nexus between poverty, childhood abuse and neglect, social and emotional dysfunction, alcohol and drug abuse and crime is so tight in the lives of many capital defendants as to form a kind of social historical profile."

Dr. Chris Mallett, Public Policy Director at Bellefaire Jewish Children's Bureau in Ohio, recently completed the most comprehensive study of traumatic experiences in the lives of death row juvenile offenders to date. He found that:

- 74% experienced family dysfunction
- 60% were victims of abuse and/or neglect
- 43% had a diagnosed psychiatric disorder
- 38% suffered from substance addictions
- 38% lived in poverty

More than 30% of death row juvenile offenders had experienced six or more distinct areas of childhood trauma with an overall average of four such experiences per offender. Most children and adolescents do not face even one of these defined areas of difficulty. Mallett also found that such mitigating evidence was presented to juries in fewer than half of the offenders' trials.

Mallett's research confirmed findings in previous studies. In 1992, researchers found that two-thirds of all juveniles sentenced to death had backgrounds of abuse, psychological disorders, low IQ, indigence, and/or substance abuse.

In 1987, an investigation into 14 juveniles on death row (40% of the total at the time) revealed that nine had major neuropsychological disorders and seven had psychotic disorders since early childhood. All but two had IQ scores under 90. Only three had average reading abilities, and another three had learned to read only after arriving on death row. Twelve reported having been physically or sexually abused, including five who were sodomized by relatives.

Juveniles Act in Desperate Ways

The turmoil often associated with adolescence can result in poor decisions and desperate behaviors. For example, studies have found that 20 to 30% of high school students consider suicide. Suicide is the third-leading cause of death among teenagers, occurring once every two hours, or over 4,000 times a year, according to the U.S. Surgeon General. Approximately 30% of youths reported using an illicit drug at least once during their lifetime, and 22.2% reported using an illicit drug within the past year.

New discoveries provide scientific confirmation that the teen years are a time of significant transition. They shed light on the mysteries of adolescence and demonstrate that adolescents have significant neurological deficiencies that result in stark limitations of judgment. Research suggests that when compounded with risk factors (neglect, abuse, poverty, etc.), these limitations can set the psychological stage for violence.

These discoveries support the assertion that adolescents are less morally culpable for their actions than competent adults and are more capable of change and rehabilitation. The ultimate punishment for minors is contrary to the idea of fairness in our justice system, which accords the greatest punishments to the most blameworthy.

This fresh understanding of adolescence does not excuse juvenile offenders from punishment for violent crime, but it clearly lessens their culpability. This concept is not new; it is why we refer to those under 18 as "minors" and "juveniles"—because, in so many respects, they are *less than adult*.

> "The immediate outcome of the Supreme Court's 5-4 decision . . . is reason enough to celebrate."

Roper Was a Step Toward the Abolition of the Death Penalty

The Nation

The Court's 2005 ruling in Roper v. Simmons *outlawing the execution of those who were under eighteen at the time they committed their crimes was trumpeted by opponents of the death penalty as yet another step in what they believed was an inevitable march toward abolition of capital punishment. In this column, the liberal news magazine* The Nation *praised the majority of the Court for publicly embracing international human rights standards by rejecting the execution of juveniles as inhumane. At the same time, the* Nation *editors warned that the Court was still wrongly attempting to save the death penalty itself by narrowing the scope of capital punishment.*

The immediate outcome of the Supreme Court's 5-to-4 decision in *Roper v. Simmons* is reason enough to celebrate: With one stroke it set aside seventy-two death sentences imposed for crimes committed by teenagers and categorically banned capital punishment for offenders under 18. The Court's powerful majority opinion—all the more notable because it was written by [President Ronald] Reagan appointee Anthony Kennedy—adds momentum to the narrowing of capital sentences and diminishing number of executions in the United States. Justice Kennedy's opinion explicitly acknowl-

The Nation, "Too Young to Die," March 21, 2005. Copyright © 2005 by The Nation Magazine/The Nation Company, Inc. Reproduced by permission.

edges teenagers' universal "vulnerability and comparative lack of control over their immediate surroundings," elaborated with a humane and scientific recognition of developmental psychology, too long absent from the death penalty debate.

But the significance of *Roper v. Simmons* goes far beyond those seventy-two cases, thanks to Justice Kennedy's unapologetic embrace of international human rights standards. Noting that the United States was the only nation left routinely imposing capital punishment on teens, Kennedy invoked "the overwhelming weight of international public opinion": a judicial glove smacked across the faces of Antonin Scalia and the whole original-intent crowd, so full of disdain for the Court's recent embrace of evolving global standards in other death penalty cases and in gay rights cases. Considering the international context of human rights, Kennedy wrote pointedly, "does not lessen our fidelity to the Constitution or our pride in its origins."

Since only a handful of nations still maintain capital punishment under any circumstances, the implication of Kennedy's remark for future death penalty cases should not be underestimated. The Court's growing willingness to listen to briefs from the EU [European Union] and retired American diplomats should cause the Bush Administration particular uneasiness as more and more cases from the "war on terror" make their way up the docket: "The overwhelming weight of international public opinion" applies as thoroughly to torture and imprisonment without charge.

Abolition of Capital Punishment Is Still Far Off

Does *Roper v. Simmons* presage abolition of capital punishment? It certainly adds momentum, as does the recent reversal of death penalty sentiment in New York's legislature. But capital punishment's shrewdest defenders—among them, perhaps, Justice Kennedy himself—now consciously seek to narrow the death penalty in order to save it. Justice Sandra Day O'Connor frets aloud about the poor quality of capital representation, and no less an execution-friendly President than George W. Bush now promotes increased spending for death-row lawyers. This isn't because of some new love of civil rights. The right needs the public clamor stirred by executions. So the smarter defenders of state killing have a strategy to dampen public doubt: join in sweeping from the table those cases most likely to make the public uneasy—children, the retarded, the provably innocent, defendants whose lawyers are drunk or asleep in court. Then shift the focus to defendants less likely to rouse sympathy: serial killers, sexual sadists, "the worst of the worst." At the same time, the Justice Department continues to use federal capital charges to introduce execution in non-death penalty states.

Roper v. Simmons is a much-deserved vindication for those lawyers who since 1989 have watched, sickened, as their teenage clients were executed. The ruling leaves an end to the American death penalty more clearly in sight. But as the goal draws closer, death penalty abolitionists must be prepared for a debate newly stripped to emotional essentials: the value of vengeance as social policy. We are still far from the moment when a majority of Supreme Court Justices, echoing their late colleague Harry Blackmun, say they will no longer "tinker with the machinery of death" and rule the death penalty, in any form, unconstitutional.

> "The Court majority once more exhibited for all to see that dazzling combination of lawlessness and moral presumption which increasingly characterizes its Bill of Rights jurisprudence."

The *Roper* Decision Was a Travesty

Robert H. Bork

Many critics strongly disagreed with the Court's 2005 ruling in Roper v. Simmons *outlawing the execution of juveniles. Many in particular objected to the Court's reliance on foreign law in arriving at its decision. Writing in the conservative* National Review, *renowned legal scholar Robert Bork denounced the Court's decision as a travesty. Specifically, he criticized the Court for disregarding the suffering of crime victims, downplaying the importance of deterrence and retribution in criminal justice, and improperly relying on international opinion. The decision, he concluded, was part of a long-standing effort by the liberal majority of the Court to attack the Constitution. Robert Bork is a former Yale Law School professor, U.S. solicitor general, and judge on the U.S. court of appeals; he is currently a distinguished fellow at the Hudson Institute and a professor at Ave Maria Law School. In 1987 he was nominated to the Supreme Court by Ronald Reagan, but he was rejected by the U.S. Senate after acrimonious confirmation hearings.*

Robert H. Bork, "Travesty Time, Again," *National Review*, March 28, 2005. Copyright © 2005 by National Review, Inc., 215 Lexington Avenue, New York, NY 10016. Reproduced by permission.

Forbidding the Execution of Juveniles

There are plenty of reasons to deplore *Roper v. Simmons*, the Supreme Court's decision that a murderer under the age of 18 when he committed his crime cannot be given the death penalty. The Court majority once more exhibited for all to see that dazzling combination of lawlessness and moral presumption which increasingly characterizes its Bill of Rights jurisprudence.

The opinion starts unpromisingly, informing us that by "protecting even those convicted of heinous crimes, the Eighth Amendment reaffirms the duty of the government to respect the dignity of all persons." Readers may wonder about the dignity of the victim. Christopher Simmons, then 17, discussed with two companions his desire to murder someone, saying they could "get away with it" because they were minors. He and a juvenile confederate broke into the house of Shirley Crook, covered her eyes and mouth, and bound her hands with duct tape. They drove her to a state park, walked her onto a bridge, tied her hands and feet together with electrical wire, completely covered her whole face with duct tape, and threw her into the Meramec River, where, helpless, she drowned. Simmons bragged about the killing to friends, telling them he had killed a woman "because the bitch seen my face." Arrested, he confessed, and was sentenced to death.

The Decision Takes Away State Sovereignty

The Supreme Court, though conceding that retribution and deterrence are valid functions of the death penalty, intoned that "we have established the propriety and affirmed the necessity of referring to 'the evolving standards of decency that mark the progress of a maturing society' to determine which punishments are so disproportionate as to be cruel and unusual." That means the justices' views evolve, which is, by definition, progress. Justice Anthony Kennedy's opinion attempted to mask this unpalatable reality by claiming that the meaning of the Eighth Amendment had changed owing to a new "national consensus" against executing under-18 killers. This assertion of a "national consensus," however, was derived from the example of just 18 states that had faced the issue of granting an exemption to juvenile murderers out of the 38 with the death penalty. This dubious escalator means that the founders who allowed such punishments fall well short of our superior understanding of decency, as do the 20 states that today permit the execution of those younger than 18. In Simmons's case, it took the Missouri legislature, the governor, a unanimous jury, and a judge to bring him to death row. All now stand branded, five to four, as morally indecent. The majority did not, and could not, explain why any state is forbidden to make a policy choice—denied its constitutional sovereignty—because other states disagree with it.

The Court Ignores the Power of Retribution

Trying its hand at psychology, the *Roper* majority argued that neither deterrence nor retribution supported the death penalty for killers under the age of 18. As for deterrence, the Court said, the likelihood that teenagers engage in cost-benefit analysis that attaches any weight to the possibility of execution is so remote as to be virtually non-existent. This in a case where the murderer counted on his minority to "get away with it." This from a Court that finds teenage girls sufficiently mature to decide on abortion without parental knowledge or consent. Retribution was discounted on the theory that young killers, apparently without exception, are less culpable than presumably more thoughtful adult murderers. The Court ignored the fact that juries, unlike the Court, do not decide such issues categorically but by evaluation of the individual and must take youth into account as one mitigating factor.

Retribution was also ruled out without considering its indispensable role in the criminal-justice system. The mixture of reprobation and expiation in retribution is sometimes required as a dramatic mark of our sense of great evil and to reinforce our respect for ourselves and the dignity of others. None of this was examined by the Court. Its steady piecemeal restriction of the death penalty—now "reserved for a narrow category of crimes and offenders"—suggests that the Court is on a path to abolish capital punishment altogether even though the Constitution four times explicitly assumes its legitimacy.

We Should Not Be Bound by Foreign Law

The most ominous aspect of *Roper*, however, is the Court majority's reliance upon foreign decisions and unratified treaties. The opinion cited "the stark reality that the United States is the only country in the world that continues to give official sanction to the juvenile death penalty," a fact the Court found "instructive" in interpreting the American Constitution. Since the nations of Europe have, among others, abolished the death penalty, the Court seems to be suggesting that we (or rather the justices) should do likewise. After all, "[w]e have previously recognized the relevance of the views of the international community in determining whether a punishment is cruel and unusual." If the meaning of a document over 200 years old can be affected by the current state of world opinion, James Madison and his colleagues labored in vain.

Article 37 of the United Nations Convention on the Rights of the Child, we are reminded, expressly prohibits capital punishment for those under 18. The United States—almost uniquely among countries—did not ratify it. Indeed, this country has never accepted any international covenant containing the prohibition in Article 37. "In sum, it is fair to say that the United States now stands alone in a world that has turned its face against the juvenile death penalty." To accept such covenants would, of course, be attempting to alter our Constitution by treaty. Perhaps that is why the Court hedged: "The opinion of the world community, while not controlling our outcome, does provide respected and significant confirmation for our own conclusions." This "underscores the centrality of those same rights within our own heritage of freedom." That comes pretty close to accepting foreign control of the American Constitution.

The Court Is Destroying the True America

What is really alarming about *Roper* and other cases citing foreign law (six justices now engage in that practice) is that the Court, in tacit coordination with foreign courts, is moving toward a global bill of rights. Neither our courts nor the foreign courts are bound by actual constitutions. Prof. Lino Graglia was quite right when he said that "the first and most important thing to know about American constitutional law is that it has virtually nothing to do with the Constitution." That is certainly the case with the Bill of Rights. From abortion to homosexual sodomy, from religion to political speech and pornography, from capital punishment to discrimination on the basis of race and sex, the Court is steadily remaking American political, social, and cultural life. As Justice Antonin Scalia once said in dissent, "Day by day, case by case, [the Court] is busy designing a Constitution for a country I do not recognize."

The courts of the United Kingdom, Canada, Israel, and almost all Western countries are doing the same thing, replacing the meaning of their charters with their own preferences. Nor are these judicial alterations random. The culture war evident in the United States is being waged internationally, both within individual nations and in international institutions and tribunals. It is a war for dominance between two moral visions of the future. One is the liberal-elite preference for radical personal autonomy and the other is the general public's desire for some greater degree of community and social authority. Elite views are fairly uniform across national boundaries, and since American and foreign judges belong to elites and respond to elite views, judge-made constitutions tend to converge. It hardly matters what particular constitutions say or were understood to mean by those who adopted them.

Judges are not, of course, the only forces for a new elite global morality. Governments and non-governmental organizations are actively promoting treaties, conventions, and new institutions (the International Criminal Court, for example) that embody their view that sovereignty and nation-states are outmoded and that we must move toward regional or even global governance. American self-government and sovereignty would be submerged in a web of international regulations. The Supreme Court, in decisions like *Roper*, adds constitutional law to the web. That is the one strand, given our current acceptance of judicial supremacy, that cannot be rejected democratically. What is clear is that foreign elites understand the importance of having the Supreme Court on their side, which is precisely why their human-rights organizations have begun filing amicus briefs urging our Supreme Court to adopt the foreign, elite view of the American Constitution.

Roper is one more reason that it is urgent that the president nominate and battle for justices who will rein in a Court run amok.

Organizations to Contact

American Civil Liberties Union (ACLU)
125 Broad St., 18th Fl., New York, NY 10004
(212) 549-2500 • fax: (212) 549-2646
Web site: www.aclu.org

The ACLU believes that capital punishment violates the Constitution's ban on cruel and unusual punishment as well as the requirements of due process and equal protection under the law.

Amnesty International USA (AI)
322 Eighth Ave., New York, NY 10001
(212) 807-8400 • fax: (212) 627-1451
Web site: www.amnesty-usa.org

Amnesty International is an independent worldwide human rights movement. AI's Program to Abolish the Death Penalty coordinates efforts to build coalitions with grassroots activists and social justice organizations working toward the elimination of the death penalty worldwide.

Canadian Coalition Against the Death Penalty (CCADP)
PO Box 38104, 550 Eglinton Ave. West
  Toronto, ONM5N 3A8 Canada
(416) 693-9112 • fax: (416) 686-1630
e-mail: info@ccadp.org
Web site: www.ccadp.org

The CCADP is a not-for-profit international human rights organization dedicated to educating the public on alternatives to the death penalty worldwide and to providing emotional and practical support to death row inmates, their families, and the families of murder victims.

Organizations to Contact

Criminal Justice Legal Foundation (CJLF)
PO Box 1199, Sacramento, CA 95816
(916) 446-0345
e-mail: cjlf@cjlf.org
Web site: www.cjlf.org

The CJLF seeks to restore a balance between the rights of crime victims and the criminally accused. The foundation supports the death penalty and works to reduce the length, complexity, and expense of appeals as well as to improve law enforcement's ability to identify and prosecute criminals.

Death Penalty Focus
870 Market St., Suite 859, San Francisco, CA 94102
(415) 243-0143 • fax: (415) 243-0994
e-mail: info@deathpenalty.org
Web site: www.deathpenalty.org

Founded in 1988, Death Penalty Focus is a nonprofit organization dedicated to the abolition of capital punishment through grassroots organization, research, and the dissemination of information about the death penalty and its alternatives.

Death Penalty Information Center (DPIC)
1326 Eighteenth St. NW, 5th Fl., Washington, DC 20036
(202) 293-6970 • fax: (202) 822-4787
e-mail: dpic@deathpenaltyinfo.org
Web site: www.deathpenaltyinfo.org

The DPIC conducts research into public opinion on the death penalty. The center believes capital punishment is discriminatory and excessively costly and that it may result in the execution of innocent persons.

Innocence Project
100 Fifth Ave., 3rd Fl., New York, NY 10011
(212) 364-5340
e-mail: info@innocenceproject.org

Web site: www.innocenceproject.org

The Innocence Project at the Benjamin N. Cardozo School of Law at Yeshiva University is a nonprofit legal clinic that handles cases in which postconviction DNA testing of evidence can yield conclusive proof of innocence. The project has been responsible for the release of hundreds of prisoners who, while innocent of the murders for which they were on trial, were convicted and sentenced to death.

Justice for All
(713) 935-9300
e-mail: info@jfa.net
Web site: www.jfa.net

Justice for All is a not-for-profit criminal justice reform organization that supports the death penalty. It publishes the monthly newsletter *Voice of Justice* and also manages the Web sites www.murdervictims.com and www.prodeathpenalty.com.

Lamp of Hope Project
PO Box 305, League City, TX 77574-0305
e-mail: ksebung@lampofhope.org
Web site: www.lampofhope.org

The project was established and is run primarily by Texas death row inmates. Its goals include educating the public about the death penalty and its alternatives and supporting victims' families by promoting healing and reconciliation.

National Center for Policy Analysis
601 Pennsylvania Ave. NW, Suite 900
  South Building, Washington, DC 20004
(202) 220-3082 • fax: (202) 220-3096
Web site: www.ncpa.org

The National Center for Policy Analysis is a nonprofit, nonpartisan public policy research organization that is in favor of stricter judicial punishment and opposes attempts to limit the death penalty. The center regularly posts pro–death penalty articles on its Web site.

National Coalition to Abolish the Death Penalty
920 Pennsylvania Ave. SE, Washington, DC 20003
(202) 543-9577 • fax: (202) 543-7798
e-mail: kjones@ncadp.org
Web site: www.ncadp.org

The National Coalition to Abolish the Death Penalty is a collection of more than 115 groups working together to stop executions in the United States. The organization compiles statistics on the death penalty and publishes information packets, pamphlets, and research materials.

National Criminal Justice Reference Service (NCJRS)
PO Box 6000, Rockville, MD 20849-6000
(301) 519-5500
Web site: www.ncjrs.gov

The National Criminal Justice Reference Service is a federally funded resource administered by the Office of Justice Programs of the U.S. Department of Justice. The nonpartisan service provides information to support research, policy, and program development around the world. The NCJRS makes available numerous capital punishment reports and statistics.

For Further Research

Books

James R. Acker, Robert M. Bohm, and Charles S. Lanier, eds., *America's Experiment with Capital Punishment: Reflections on the Past, Present, and Future of the Ultimate Penal Sanction*. Durham, NC: Carolina Academic Press, 1998.

Mary Welek Atwood, *Evolving Standards of Decency: Popular Culture and Capital Punishment*. New York: Peter Lang, 2004.

Stuart Banner, *The Death Penalty: An American History*. Cambridge, MA: Harvard University Press, 2002.

Hugo Adam Bedau, ed., *The Death Penalty in America: Current Controversies*. New York: Oxford University Press, 1997.

———, *Killing as Punishment: Reflections on the Death Penalty in America*. Boston: Northeastern University Press, 2004.

Ronald W. Conley, Ruth Luckasson, and George N. Bouthilet, eds., *The Criminal Justice System and Mental Retardation*. Baltimore: Paul H. Brooks, 1992.

David R. Dow, *Executed on a Technicality: Lethal Injustice on America's Death Row*. Boston: Beacon, 2005.

Herbert H. Haines, *Against Capital Punishment: The Anti–Death Penalty Movement in America, 1972–1994*. New York: Oxford University Press, 1996.

Barry Latzer, ed., *Death Penalty Cases: Leading United States Supreme Court Cases on Capital Punishment*. Woburn, MA: Butterworth-Heinemann, 1997.

Evan J. Mandery, *Capital Punishment: A Balanced Examination*. Sudbury, MA: Jones and Bartlett, 2005.

Kent S. Miller and Michael L. Radelet, *Executing the Mentally Ill: The Criminal Justice System and the Case of Alvin Ford*. Newbury Park, CA: Sage, 1993.

Laura E. Randa, ed., *Society's Final Solution: A History and Discussion of the Death Penalty*. New York: University Press of America, 1997.

Emily Fabrycki Reed, *The Penry Penalty: Capital Punishment and Offenders with Mental Retardation*. Lanham, MD: University Press of America, 1993.

Austin Sarat, *When the State Kills: Capital Punishment and the American Condition*. Princeton, NJ: Princeton University Press, 2002.

Victor Streib, ed., *A Capital Punishment Anthology*. Cincinnati: Anderson, 1993.

Bryan Vila and Cynthia Morris, eds., *Capital Punishment in the United States: A Documentary History*. Westport, CT: Greenwood, 1997.

Periodicals

Debating the Death Penalty

Alan Berlow, "The Broken Machinery of Death," *American Prospect*, July 30, 2001.

Walter Berns, "Where Are the Death Penalty Critics Today?" *Wall Street Journal*, June 11, 2001.

Anne Coulter, "The Last Guys 'Proved Innocent,'" *Jewish World Review*, June 27, 2000.

Samuel R. Gross, "Still Unfair, Still Arbitrary—but Do We Care?" *Ohio Northern University Law Review*, vol. 26, 2000.

Ramesh Ponnuru, "Not So Innocent: The Death Penalty: An Argument Continued," *National Review*, October 1, 2002.

Carol Steiker, "Things Fall Apart, but the Center Holds: The Supreme Court and the Death Penalty," *New York University Law Review*, vol. 77, 2002.

Carol Steiker and Jordan Steiker, "Sober Second Thoughts: Reflections on Two Decades of Constitutional Regulation of Capital Punishment," *Harvard Law Review*, vol. 109, 1995.

Andrew Stephen, "Americans Show Signs of Killer Fatigue," *New Statesman*, June 18, 2001.

Stuart Taylor Jr., "The Death Penalty Debate Intensifies," *Newsweek*, June 11, 2001.

Scott Turow, "To Kill or Not to Kill: Coming to Terms with Capital Punishment," *New Yorker*, January 6, 2003.

Charles Wheeler, "The Right to Life," *Spectator*, February 17, 2001.

Richard Willing, "Death Penalty Gains Unusual Defenders," *USA Today*, January 6, 2003.

Juveniles and the Death Penalty

Sasha Abramsky, "Taking Juveniles Off Death Row," *American Prospect*, July 2004.

Bruce Bower, "Teen Brains on Trial: The Science of Neural Development Tangles with the Juvenile Death Penalty," *Science News*, May 8, 2004.

Mitchel Brim, "A Sneak Preview into How the Court Took Away a State's Right to Execute Sixteen and Seventeen Year Old Juveniles: The Threat of Execution Will No Longer Save an Innocent Victim's Life," *Denver University Law Review*, Vol. 82, 2005.

James A. Cooley, "Supreme Inaccuracies," *National Review*, July 9, 2002.

Arline Kaplan, "When Is It 'Cruel and Unusual Punishment'? Supreme Court Bans Juvenile Death Penalty," *Psychiatric Times*, May 1, 2005.

Jeffrey Rosen, "Juvenile Logic," *New Republic*, March 21, 2005.

Victor L. Streib, "Executing Juvenile Offenders: The Ultimate Denial of Juvenile Justice," *Stanford Law and Policy Review*, Vol. 14, 2003.

Mental Retardation and the Death Penalty

Jonathan Alter, "Between the Lines Online: Supreme Misgivings," *Newsweek*, July 12, 2002.

Economist, "The Ebbing of Death," June 29, 2002.

Lancet, "A Step Forward for Humanity?" March 16, 2002.

Adam Liptak, "New Challenge for Courts: How to Define Retardation," *New York Times*, March 14, 2004.

Margaret Talbot, "The Executioner's I.Q. Test," *New York Times Magazine*, June 29, 2003.

Race, Class, and the Death Penalty

Amnesty International, "Death by Discrimination: The Continuing Role of Race in Capital Cases," April 24, 2003. http://web.amnesty.org.

Roger Clegg, "The Color of Death," *National Review*, June 11, 2001.

Scott W. Howe, "The Futile Quest for Racial Neutrality in Capital Selection and the Eighth Amendment Argument for Abolition Based on Unconscious Racial Discrimination," *William & Mary Law Review*, April 2004.

Gene Koretz, "Equality? Not on Death Row," *Business Week*, June 30, 2003.

Charles J. Ogletree Jr., "Black Man's Burden: Race and the Death Penalty in America?" *Oregon Law Review*, Vol. 81, 2002.

Christina Swarns, "The Uneven Scales of Capital Justice: How Race and Class Affect Who Ends Up on Death Row," *American Prospect*, July 2004.

Web Sites

The Clark County Prosecuting Attorney: The Death Penalty (www.clarkprosecutor.org). Web site of the prosecuting attorney of Clark County, Indiana; slanted pro–death penalty, but contains hundreds of links to stories, articles, and reports representing multiple sides of the capital punishment debate.

Death Penalty Information Center (www.deathpenaltyinfo.org). Informational Web site with links to death penalty curricula and resources about capital punishment; slanted against the death penalty.

FindLaw (www.findlaw.com). Online tool for searching for cases and legal codes.

The International Justice Project (www.internationaljusticeproject.org). Web site of an organization that favors abolishing the death penalty; promotes increased application of international law and human rights standards to questions about capital punishment.

The OYEZ Project (www.oyez.org). An online, multimedia archive and guide to the Supreme Court and to many Court decisions; includes recordings of oral arguments.

Index

adolescents
    brain development in, 160–62
    physical changes of, 164
    see also juvenile offenders
American Association on Mental Retardation (AAMR), 116, 117–18, 126
American Bar Association (ABA), 159
American Civil Liberties Union (ACLU), 78, 176
American Psychiatric Society (APA), 115–18
American support for death penalty. *see* public opinion
Amnesty International, 92, 176
Amsterdam, Anthony, 88
antisocial personality disorder, 145–46
arbitrariness
    Court objections to, 50–51
    death penalty is imposed with, 27–29, 33–38, 50–51, 77–83, 90
    is hard to prove, 51–52
    murder convictions highlighting, 80–81
    sentencing guidelines to reduce, 53–54, 66–69
Arenella, Peter, 124
Atkins, Daryl, 94–96, 114, 124, 134
Atkins v. Virginia, 16, 141, 160
    case overview, 94–96
    dissenting opinion in, 105–12
    majority opinion in, 97–104
    national consensus and, 151–52
    raises troubling moral issues, 123–30
    was misuse of psychiatry, 113–22
    will destigmatize the mentally retarded, 131–36

Benjamin, Charles, 138
Bersoff, Donald, 132–33
Binder, Renee, 116
Black, Charles L. Jr., 64
Blackmun, Harry, 12, 22, 58, 169
Bodiker, David, 124, 129–30
Bork, Robert H., 170
brain research, 160–64
Brennan, William J. Jr., 24, 58
Breyer, Stephen, 16
Burger, Warren, 39
    Furman opinion of, 22, 39–48
    Gregg opinion of, 58
Bush, George W., 169

Callins, Bruce, 12
Canadian Coalition Against the Death Penalty (CCADP), 176
capital punishment. *see* death penalty
childhood abuse, 164–65
Clinton, Bill, 16
Coker v. Georgia, 14, 91, 106, 147
community standards, 61–62
Constitution
    remaking of, 174–75
    see also Eighth Amendment; Fourteenth Amendment
crime, severity of, and punishment, 65–66
Criminal Justice Legal Foundation (CJLF), 177
Crocker, Phyllis L., 164–65
Crook, Shirley, 138
Croser, Doree'n, 116
cruel and unusual punishment
    death penalty is, 24–34, 70–76
    con, 39–48

execution of mentally retarded is, 97–104
  con, 105–12
culpability
  of juveniles, 142–44, 154–55, 159–66
  of mentally retarded, 110–12, 126–27, 130, 133–34

Davis, Kenneth C., 54
death penalty
  arbitrariness of, 27–29, 33–38, 50–51, 77–83, 90
    is hard to prove, 51–52
    sentencing guidelines to reduce, 53–54, 66–69
  as deterrent, 45–46, 64–65
    does not apply to juveniles, 143–44, 172
    does not apply to mentally retarded, 102–3
    is inadequate justification, 73–74
    is not proven, 91–92
  as retribution, 62–64, 72–75, 91–92
    does not apply to juveniles, 143–44
    does not apply to mentally retarded, 102–3
  for juveniles
    is unconstitutional, 140–48
    no national consensus against, 149–58
    world opinion on, 139, 146–48, 156–57, 168
  for the mentally retarded
  history of, in U.S., 41–42
  is constitutional, 37, 39–48, 59–69
    con, 24–34, 70–76
    is excessive punishment, 97–104
  is not unconstitutional, 105–12
  public support for, 43–44, 58, 62–64, 80
    is declining, 89–90
    is insufficient reason, 74–75
  racial bias in, 51–52, 79–82, 90–91
  Roper was step toward abolition of, 167–69
  severity of, 65–66
  violates human dignity, 24–34
Death Penalty Focus, 177
Death Penalty Information Center, 124, 177
death penalty jurisprudence, history of, 12–18
death penalty statutes, after *Furman*, 14, 49–54
death row inmates
  juvenile, 165
  mentally retarded, 125, 128–29
deterrent effect, 45–46, 64–65
  is inadequate justification, 73–74
  for juveniles, 143–44, 172
  for mentally retarded, 102–3
  is not proven, 91–92
Dieter, Richard, 124
discretion in sentencing
  by prosecutors, is mercy, 83
  reducing, can ensure fairness, 66–69
  should be limited, 52–53
discrimination
  vs. mercy, 83
  in sentencing, 51–52, 79–82, 90–91
  see also arbitrariness
Douglas, William O., 22

Index

Eddings v. Oklahoma, 154–55
Eighth Amendment
    acceptance of society and, 75
    arbitrary punishment and, 50–51
    death penalty does not violate, 41–42, 60–61
    execution of mentally retarded and, 98, 105–6, 110
    juvenile executions and, 139, 141, 143, 156–57, 171–72
    retribution and, 45
    uncertain language of, 40
    see also cruel and unusual punishment
Enmund v. Florida, 102, 103, 147
Everington, Caroline, 130

Farmer, Millard, 79, 82
Fifth Amendment, 61
Ford v. Wainwright, 15–16, 106
Fourteenth Amendment, 35
    death penalty does not violate, 60–61
    juvenile executions and, 148
Furman v. Georgia, 13–14, 85, 88
    Brennan opinion in, 24–34
    Burger opinion in, 39–48
    case overview, 21–22
    new death penalty laws after, 49–54
    Stewart opinion in, 35–38, 64

Georgia
    death sentences in, 82
    number of executions in, 79
Giedd, Jay, 162
Ginsburg, Ruth Bader, 16
global morality, 174–75
Godfrey v. Georgia, 15, 102, 111
Goldberg, Arthur, 85
Graglia, Lino, 174
Greenspan, Stephen, 128

Gregg v. Georgia, 14
    case overview, 56–58
    Marshall opinion in, 70–76
    on justifications for death penalty, 110–11
    Stewart opinion in, 59–69, 92
    was correct ruling, 84–86
    con, 87–92
Greider, William, 77
guided discretion statutes, 14
Gur, Ruben C., 162

Harmelin v. Michigan, 110
Harvard Law Review, 49
Huff, Bryant, 79–80, 83
human brain, 160–65
human dignity, death penalty violates, 24–34
human rights, international opinion and, 168, 174–75

Illinois, 90
Innocence Project, 177–78
insane offenders, execution of, 15–16
intelligence
    tests for, 119–21, 123–24, 127–28
    vs. morality, 127
international opinion. *see* world opinion
IQ scores
    unreliability of, 119–21, 123–24, 127–28
    variations in, 130

Johnson v. Texas, 142, 154
Jurek, Jerry Lane, 86
Jurek v. Texas, 14
jury guidelines, can ensure fairness, 66–69
Justice for All, 178

juvenile executions
  are unconstitutional, 140–48
  no national consensus against, 149–58
  world opinion on, 139, 146–48, 156–57, 168
juvenile offenders
  are different than adults, 142
  culpability of, 142–44, 154–55, 159–66
  dividing line between adults and, 155–56
  mitigating factors and, 144–46
  Roper v. Simmons decision on, 16, 138–39

Kansas, 107
Kennedy, Anthony, 140
  liberalism of, 16
  Roper opinion of, 139, 140–48, 167–68
Keyes, Denis, 126, 129

Lamp of Hope Project, 178
Lee, Rob, 125
Legal Defense Fund, 78
Lewis, Melvin, 164
life without parole sentences, 91–92
Lockett v. Ohio, 14, 104, 141

Mallet, Chris, 165
mandatory death sentences, 14
Marshall, Thurgood, 58, 70
mental health professionals, capital punishment process and, 121–22
mentally ill, execution of, 15–16
mentally retarded
  Atkins ruling on, 16, 94–96
  will destigmatize, 131–36
  characteristics of, 100–102, 115–16
  classification of, 127–30
  culpability of, 110–12, 126–27, 130, 133–35
  diagnosis of, 115–22, 123–24
  execution of
    is excessive punishment, 97–104
    is not unconstitutional, 105–12
  levels of, 128–29
  make poor witnesses, 103–4, 112
mercy, 83
Meyers, Gregory, 129
mitigating factors
  age as, 141
  as evidence, 14
  childhood abuse as, 164–65
  in juvenile cases, 144–46
morality, vs. intelligence, 127
moral outrage, death penalty as expression of, 74
Mossman, Douglas, 113, 127
murder convictions, examples of arbitrariness in, 80–81

Nation, The, 167
National Center for Policy Analysis, 178
National Coalition to Abolish the Death Penalty, 179
national consensus. *see* public opinion
National Criminal Justice Reference Service (NCJRS), 179
National Review, 84
Nebraska, 90
New Hampshire, 90
New York, 107

Index

O'Connor, Sandra Day, 18, 139, 149, 169
O'Neil v. Vermont, 26

pain, infliction of, 32
Penry, John, 133, 134–35
Penry v. Lynaugh, 16, 94, 99, 104, 106, 114, 115
People v. Anderson, 32
Powell, Lewis F.
    Furman opinion of, 22
    Gregg opinion of, 57–58
prisoners, rights of, 32–33
Proffitt v. Florida, 14
prosecutor's discretion, in death penalty cases, 82–83
psychiatrists, role of, 121–22
psychiatry, Atkins was misuse of, 113–22
psychologists, role of, 121–22
public opinion
    is insufficient reason for death penalty, 74–75
    is not against execution of juveniles, 149–58
    on execution of mentally retarded, 107–9, 115
    supporting death penalty, 43–44, 58, 61–62, 80
        is declining, 89–90
        is insufficient reason, 74–75
    see also world opinion
punishment
    arbitrary, 27–29, 33–34, 50–51
    severity of, in relation to crime committed, 65–66
    see also cruel and unusual punishment

racial bias. *see* discrimination
Radelet, Michael L., 87
rape, death penalty in cases of, 14
Reagan, Ronald, 16

Rehnquist, William, 18
    Atkins opinion of, 95
    Furman opinion of, 22
    Gregg opinion of, 58
    Roper opinion of, 139
religious views, on death penalty, 89
retribution
    death penalty as, 62–64, 72–75, 91–92
        does not apply to juveniles, 143–44
        does not apply to mentally retarded, 102–3
    power of, 172–73
Roberts v. Louisiana, 14, 73
Robinson v. California, 27, 29, 30
Rompilla v. Beard, 16–17
Roper v. Simmons, 16
    case overview, 138–39
    criticism of, 170–75
    dissenting opinion in, 149–58
    majority opinion in, 140–48
    significance of, 167–69
Ryan, George, 90

Scalia, Antonin, 12, 105
    Atkins opinion by, 95, 105–12, 113–14
    on recent death penalty decisions, 17–18
    on remaking of Constitution, 174
    Roper opinion of, 139
sentencing guidelines, can ensure fairness, 53–54, 66–69
Simmons, Christopher, 138–39, 145, 171
Slobogin, Christopher, 131
social standards. *see* "standards of decency" argument
sociopathy, 146
Solesbee v. Balkcom, 32
Southern Poverty Law Center, 79

189

Sowell, Elizabeth, 161
"standards of decency" argument, 61–62, 88–90
    execution of mentally retarded and, 98–100, 106–9, 115
    juvenile executions and, 138, 171–72
Stanford v. Kentucky, 16, 106, 139, 141, 150, 152
state legislatures
    dealing with issue of mental retardation, 99–100
    on juvenile execution, 151–53
    rethinking of death penalty by, 46–48
Stevens, John Paul, 97
    Atkins opinion of, 94–95, 97–104
    Gregg opinion of, 57–58
Stewart, Potter, 13, 35, 59
    Furman opinion of, 22, 35–38, 64
    Gregg opinion of, 57–69, 92
suicide, 166
Supreme Court decisions. *see specific decisions*

Talbot, Margaret, 123
teenagers. *see* adolescents; juvenile offenders
Thomas, Clarence, 18, 95, 139
Thompson v. Oklahoma, 16, 143, 144, 146

Trop v. Dulles, 25–27, 30–32, 43, 98, 106

United Nations Convention on the Rights of the Child, 147, 173
United States
    public opinion in. *see* public opinion
    as sole executioner of juveniles, 146–48

Warren, Earl, 41, 43, 98
Weems v. United States, 26, 27, 30, 98
White, Byron R.
    Furman opinion of, 22
    Gregg opinion of, 58
white victims, death sentences in cases of, 82
Wilkerson v. Utah, 27
Witherspoon v. Illinois, 67
Woodson v. North Carolina, 14
world opinion
    on death penalty, 89
    on execution of mentally retarded, 109
    on juvenile execution, 139, 146–48, 156–57, 168
    U.S. should not be bound by, 173–74

Yurgelun-Todd, Deborah, 162